WHAT BELONGS TO YOU

WHAT BELONGS TO YOU

GARTH GREENWELL

PICADOR

First published 2016 by Farrar, Straus and Giroux

First published in the UK 2016 by Picador
an imprint of Pan Macmillan
20 New Wharf Road, London N1 9RR
Associated companies throughout the world
www.panmacmillan.com

ISBN 978-1-4472-8051-4

Part I of *What Belongs to You* was originally published, in a very different form,
as a novella, *Mitko*, in June 2011 by the Miami University Press.

1 3 5 7 9 8 6 4 2

A CIP catalogue record for this book is available from the British Library.

Printed by CPI Group (UK) Ltd, Croydon, CR0 4YY

Visit **www.picador.com** to read more about all our books
and to buy them. You will also find features, author interviews and
news of any author events, and you can sign up for e-newsletters
so that you're always first to hear about our new releases.

*For Alan Pierson and Max Freeman
and for Luis Muñoz*

I

MITKO

That my first encounter with Mitko B. ended in a betrayal, even a minor one, should have given me greater warning at the time, which should in turn have made my desire for him less, if not done away with it completely. But warning, in places like the bathrooms at the National Palace of Culture, where we met, is like some element coterminous with the air, ubiquitous and inescapable, so that it becomes part of those who inhabit it, and thus part and parcel of the desire that draws us there. Even as I descended the stairs I heard his voice, which like the rest of him was too large for those subterranean rooms, spilling out of them as if to climb back into the bright afternoon that, though it was mid-October, had nothing autumnal about it; the grapes that hung ripe from vines throughout the city burst warm still in one's mouth. I was surprised to hear someone talking so freely in a place where, by unstated code, voices seldom rose above a whisper. At the bottom of the stairs I paid my fifty stotinki to an old woman who looked up at me from her booth, her expression unreadable as she took the coins; with her other hand she clutched a shawl against the chill that was constant here, whatever the season. Only as I neared the end of the corridor did I hear a second voice, not raised like the first, but answering in a low murmur. The voices came from the second of the bathroom's three chambers, where they might have belonged to men washing their hands had the sound of water accompanied them. I paused in the outermost room, examining myself in the mirrors lining its walls as I listened to their conversation, though I couldn't understand a word. There was only one reason for men to be standing there, the bathrooms at NDK (as the Palace is called) are well enough hidden and have such a reputation that they're hardly used for anything else; and yet as I turned into the room this explanation seemed at odds with the demeanor of the man who claimed my attention, which was cordial and brash, entirely public in that place of intense privacies.

He was tall, thin but broad-shouldered, with the close-cropped military cut of hair popular among certain young men in Sofia, who affect a hypermasculine style and an air of criminality. I hardly noticed the man he was with, who was shorter, deferential, with bleached blond hair and a denim jacket from the pockets of which he never removed his hands. It was the larger man who turned toward me with apparently friendly interest, free of predation or fear, and though I was taken aback I found myself smiling in response. He greeted me with an elaborate rush of words, at which I could only shake my head in bemusement as I grasped the large hand he held out, offering as broken apology and defense the few phrases I had practiced to numbness. His smile widened when he realized I was a foreigner, revealing a chipped front tooth, the jagged seam of which (I would learn) he worried obsessively with his index finger in moments of abstraction. Even at arm's length, I could smell the alcohol that emanated not so much from his breath as from his clothes and hair; it explained his freedom in a place that, for all its license, was bound by such inhibition, and explained too the peculiarly innocent quality of his gaze, which was intent but unthreat-

ening. He spoke again, cocking his head to one side, and in
a pidgin of Bulgarian, English, and German, we established
that I was American, that I had been in his city for a few
weeks and would stay at least a year, that I was a teacher at the
American College, that my name was more or less unpronounceable in his language.

Throughout our halting conversation, there was no acknowledgment of the strange location of our encounter or
of the uses to which it was almost exclusively put, so that
speaking to him I felt an anxiety made up of equal parts
desire and unease at the mystery of his presence and purpose. There was a third man there as well, who entered and
exited the farthest stall several times, looking earnestly at us
but never approaching or speaking a word. Finally, after we
had reached the end of our introductions and after this third
man entered his stall again, closing the door behind him,
Mitko (as I knew him now) pointed toward him and gave me
a look of great significance, saying *Iska*, he wants, and then
making a lewd gesture the meaning of which was clear. Both
he and his companion, whom he referred to as *brat mi* and
who hadn't spoken since I arrived, laughed at this, looking
at me as if to include me in the joke, though of course I was
as much an object of their ridicule as the man listening to
them from inside his stall. I was so eager to be one of their
party that almost without thinking I smiled and wagged my
head from side to side, in the gesture that signifies here both
agreement or affirmation and a certain wonder at the vagaries
of the world. But I saw in the glance they exchanged that this
attempt to associate with them only increased the distance
between us. Wanting to regain my footing, and after pausing
to arrange the necessary syllables in my head (which seldom,
despite these efforts, emerge as they should, even now when
I'm told that I speak *hubavo* and *pravilno*, when I see surprise
at my proficiency in a language that hardly anyone bothers

to learn who hasn't learned it already), I asked him what he was doing there, in that chill room with its impression of damp. Above us it felt like summer still, the plaza was full of light and people, some of them, riding skateboards or in-line skates or elaborately tricked-out bicycles, the same age as these men.

Mitko looked at his friend, whom he referred to as his brother although they were not brothers, and then the friend moved toward the outer door and Mitko drew his wallet out of his back pocket. He opened it and took out a small square packet of glossy paper, a page torn from a magazine and folded over many times. He unfolded this page carefully, his hands shaking slightly, balancing it to keep whatever loose material was inside from falling to the dampness and filth on which we stood. I guessed what he would reveal, of course; my only surprise was at how little he had, a mere crumble of leaves. Ten leva, he said, and then added that he and his friend and I, the three of us, might smoke it together. He didn't seem disappointed when I refused this offer; he just folded his page up carefully again and replaced it in his pocket. But he didn't leave, either, as I had feared he might. I wanted him to stay, even though over the course of our conversation, which moved in such fits and starts and which couldn't have lasted more than five or ten minutes, it had become difficult to imagine the desire I increasingly felt for him having any prospect of satisfaction. For all his friendliness, as we spoke he had seemed in some mysterious way to withdraw from me; the longer we avoided any erotic proposal the more finally he seemed unattainable, not so much because he was beautiful, although I found him beautiful, as for some still more forbidding quality, a kind of bodily sureness or ease that suggested freedom from doubts and self-gnawing, from any squeamishness about existence. He had about him a sense simply of accepting his right to a measure of the world's beneficence, even as so clearly it had been withheld him. He looked at his friend, who hadn't moved to rejoin us after Mitko hid away his tiny stash, and after they exchanged another glance the friend turned his back to us, not so much guarding the door anymore, I felt, as offering us a certain privacy. Mitko looked at me again, friendly still but with a new intensity, and then he tilted his head slightly and moved one hand over his crotch. I couldn't help but look down, of course, as I couldn't restrain the excitement I'm sure he saw when I met his gaze again. He rubbed the first three fingers of his other hand together, making the universal sign for money. There was nothing in his manner of seduction, no show of desire at all; what he offered was a transaction, and again he showed no disappointment when reflexively and without hesitation I said no to him. It was the answer I had always given to such proposals (which are inevitable in the places I frequent), not out of any moral conviction but out of pride, a pride that had weakened in recent years, as I realized I was being shifted by the passage of time from one category of erotic object to another. But as soon as I uttered the word I regretted it, as Mitko shrugged and dropped his hand from his crotch, smiling as if it had all been a joke. And then, since he did finally turn to leave with his friend, nodding in goodbye, I called out *Chakai chakai chakai*, wait wait wait, repeating the word quickly and in the precise inflection I had heard an old woman use at an intersection one afternoon when a stray dog began to wander into traffic. Mitko turned back at once, as docile as if our transaction had already taken place; maybe in his mind it was already a sure thing, as it was in mine, though I pretended to be skeptical of the goods on offer, trying to assert some mastery over the overwhelming excitement I felt. I looked down at his crotch and then back up, saying *Kolko ti e*, how big are you, the standard phrase, always the first question in the Internet chat rooms I used. Mitko didn't say anything in response, he smiled and stepped into a stall and unbuttoned his fly, and my pretense of hesitation fell away as I realized I would pay whatever price he wanted. I took a step toward him, reaching out as if to claim those goods right away, I've always been a terrible negotiator or haggler, my desire is immediately legible, but Mitko buttoned himself back up, raising a hand to hold me off. I thought it was payment he wanted, but instead he stepped around me, telling me to wait, and returned to the line of porcelain sinks, all of them cracked and stained. Then, with a bodily candor I ascribed to drunkenness but would learn was an inalienable trait, he pulled the long tube of his cock free from his jeans and leaned over the bowl of the sink to wash it, skinning it back and wincing at water that only comes out cold. It was some time before he was satisfied, the first sign of a fastidiousness that would never cease to surprise me, given his poverty and the tenuous circumstances in which he lived.

When he returned I asked his price for the act I wanted, which was ten leva until I unfolded my wallet and found only twenty-leva notes, one of which he eagerly claimed. Really what did it matter, the sums were almost equally meaningless to me; I would have paid twice as much, and twice as much again, which isn't to suggest that I had particularly ample resources, but that his body seemed almost infinitely dear. It was astonishing to me that any number of these soiled bills could make that body available, that after the simplest of exchanges I could reach out for it and find it in my grasp. I placed my hands under the tight shirt he wore, and he gently pushed me back so that he could remove it, undoing each of its buttons and then hanging it carefully on the hook of the stall door behind him. He was thinner than I expected, less defined, and the hair that covered his torso had been shaved to bare stubble, so that for the first time I realized how young he was (I would learn he was twenty-three) as he stood boyish and exposed before me. He motioned me forward again with the exaggerated courtesy some drunk men assume, which can precede, the thought even in my excitement was never far, equally exaggerated outbursts of rage. Mitko surprised me then by leaning forward and laying his mouth on mine, kissing me generously, unrestrainedly, and though I hadn't done anything to invite such contact it was welcome and I sucked eagerly on his tongue, which was antiseptic with alcohol. I knew he was performing a desire he didn't feel, and really I think he was drunk past the possibility of desire. But then there's something theatrical in all our embraces, I think, as we weigh our responses against those we perceive or project; always we desire too much or not enough, and compensate accordingly. I was performing too, pretending to believe that his show of passion was a genuine response to my own desire, about which there was nothing feigned. As if he sensed these thoughts he pressed me more tightly to him, and for the first time I caught, beneath the more powerful and nearly overwhelming smell of alcohol, his own scent, which would be the greatest source of the pleasure I took from him and which I would seek out (at his neck and crotch, beneath his arms) at each of our meetings. It put an end to my thinking, I lifted one of his hands above his head, breaking our kiss to press my face into the pit of his arm (he shaved there too, the skin was rough against my tongue), sucking at his scent as if taking some necessary nourishment at an inadequate source. And then I sank to my knees and took him in my mouth.

A few minutes later, well before he had given me what I was owed, the obligation he took on when he took a soiled twenty-leva note from my hand, Mitko made a strange loud sound and tensed himself, placing both of his palms flat against the sides of the stall. It was a poor performance of an orgasm, if that's what it was, not least because for the few minutes I had sucked him he had shown no response at all. *Chakai*, I said to him in protest as he pulled away, *iskam oshte*, I want more, but he didn't relent, he smiled at me and motioned me back, still courteous as he put on the shirt he had hung so carefully behind him. I watched him helplessly, still kneeling, as he called out to his friend, whom he called again *brat mi* and who called back to him from the outer chamber. Maybe he saw that I was angry, and wanted to remind me he wasn't alone. Straightening his clothes, running his hands down his torso to settle them properly on his frame, he smiled without guile, as if maybe he did feel he had given me what he owed. Then he unlatched the door and pulled it shut again behind him. As I knelt there, still tasting the metallic trace of sinkwater from his skin, I felt my anger lifting as I realized that my pleasure wasn't lessened by his absence, that what was surely a betrayal (we had our contract, though it had never been signed, never set in words at all) had only refined our encounter, allowing him to become more vividly present to me even as I was left alone on my stained knees, and allowing me, with all the freedom of fantasy, to make of him what I would.

I sought Mitko out repeatedly over the next weeks, and after our third or fourth encounter I decided to invite him to my apartment. I wanted him to myself, free of the audience we so frequently had at NDK, where men would hover outside the stall door or press their ears to its walls, as I had done also when I found myself among the unchosen. I wanted more time and more privacy with Mitko, but I was uneasy, too, and recognized the foolishness of bringing this near stranger into my home. I remembered the warning of a man who had invited me, after we met in the bathroom, to have coffee with him in the large café in the main building of the Palace. These boys, he said to me, you can't trust them, they will find out about you, they will tell your work, your friends, they will rob you—and indeed I had been robbed, once successfully and once I caught a young man's hand as he withdrew it from my pocket, after which he stared wild-eyed at me, the poor boy, and fled. The rest of this man's warning fell on deaf ears, as I had very little to lose from such revelations— no one would feel betrayed, nothing would be marred by the telling of secrets I hardly bothered to hide; I've never been good at concealing anything, the whole bent of my nature is toward confession. Mitko and I had already had sex; it was afterward, sitting on a bench in the sunlight, which was still warm though it was November now, the grapes had shriveled on their vines, that I decided to return to the bathrooms below and offer him my proposal. We set up a date for the following evening, and his eyes lit up at the sight of my phone, which I pulled out for the first time in his presence to take down his number. He snatched it from me, only after it was in his hand saying *Mozhe li*, may I, and as I watched him scroll through its various features and screens, I remembered the warning I had been given.

But this unease wasn't enough to dissuade me, and the next afternoon after classes I hurried downtown. We met again at NDK, where I found him in a huddle with three or four other men at the wall farthest from the entrance. They scattered when I appeared, though I didn't approach them but stood awkwardly at the threshold. Mitko, who had his back to me, turned and smiled, offering me his hand and at the same time directing me out of the room and away from his friends (if they were his friends), leading me toward the plaza above. As we climbed the long staircase, moving away from those rooms that had always seemed too small for him, his frame and voice and friendliness all hemmed in by the damp tile of the walls, I felt, along with the excitement I had anticipated, an entirely unexpected happiness. *Kak si*, I asked as we walked through the park at NDK, how are you, and he showed me the knuckles of his right hand, which were skinned and raw, the wounds still fresh. He said that he had gotten into a fight with another man down below, though the reasons for it remained unclear to me. I took his hand in mine for a moment, looking at the little wounds that made him at once fierce and damaged, and I imagined how I would salve them, rubbing them with ointment and then pressing them to my lips. But this was a kind of tenderness that had never been part of our encounters and that was especially out of place now, as he reenacted his fight with quick jabs in the air. We walked down Vasil Levski Boulevard, Mitko's long legs devouring the pavement as I struggled to keep up, and he talked the whole way, only bits of what he said comprehensible to me. For the first time I asked him where he lived and he answered *S priyateli*, with friends, a term that he used often and that I was never sure how to interpret, since in addition to its usual meanings Mitko used it to refer to his clients. It became clear to me, as I struggled to understand his stream of talk (frequently punctuated with *razbirash li*, do you understand?), that Mitko shuttled between places, sometimes sleeping with these friends, sometimes walking the streets until morning. When the weather was bad, he could go to a small garret room to which a friend had given him a key (*Edna mansarda*, he said, making the shape of a roof with his hands), where there was a mattress but no heat or running water.

Speaking of these things seemed to make Mitko uneasy, and he changed the subject by saying that, though I had found him at NDK, where he had spent much of the day, he had nevertheless been saving himself for our evening together. He looked at me sidelong as he said this (*Razbirash li?*) and I felt myself flush with excitement. Mitko seemed eager, too, full of an energy that propelled him forward, and as we walked down Vasil Levski toward Graf Ignatief, crossing innumerable side streets and alleyways, more than once I had to grab his arm and, saying to him again *Chakai chakai chakai*, pull him back from oncoming traffic. When we turned onto Graf Ignatief, he stopped in front of the many electronics stores and pawnshops, evaluating the products laid out in their windows. I was surprised by how much he knew about these phones and tablets, his monologues punctuated by English words for the various devices' specs, pixels and memory cards and battery life, information he must have gleaned from the advertisements and brochures he picked up wherever they were offered. I tried to hurry him along, impatient to get home and uneasy at what seemed more and more like hints, especially when Mitko told me that his current phone, a model he clearly hoped to upgrade, was a gift from one of his friends. This word, *podaruk*, gift, would recur again and again in Mitko's conversation that evening, applied, it seemed, to nearly everything he owned.

Finally we came to the end of Graf Ignatief, and as we approached the small river that circles central Sofia, really little more than a drainage ditch, Mitko said *Chakai malko*, wait a little, and stepped off the sidewalk toward the sparse vegetation at the river's bank. I walked on a few steps, then turned to look back at him, though I could barely make him out (it was dark now, the autumn night had fallen as we walked) as he stood at the bank to relieve himself into the water. He seemed entirely unconcerned by the passersby, the heavy traffic on one of Sofia's busiest streets; and when he caught me watching him, he stuck his tongue out and wagged his cock in his hand, sending his piss in high arcs over the water, where it glimmered in the lights of oncoming cars. It was a gesture so innocent, so full of childlike irreverence, that I found myself smiling stupidly back at him, filled with a sense of goodwill that buoyed me toward the metro station and our short commute. There was only one metro line in Sofia (though more were planned and great trenches had been gouged in neighborhoods throughout the city), and during peak hours it seemed as though the entire population were shuttling underground, alternately swallowed and disgorged through the closing doors. There were no seats on the Mladost train, and Mitko and I were separated from each other, standing finally some distance apart in the press of bodies. Mitko studied the maps above each set of doors, watching the stations light up as we passed them, but every now and then he glanced at me, as if to make sure I was still there or that my attention was still fixed on him, and his look now wasn't innocent, anything but; it was a look that singled me out, a look full of promise, and under its heat I felt myself gripped yet again by both pleasure and embarrassment, and by an excitement so terrible I had to look away.

When we emerged at the subway's last stop, Mladost 1, spilling with the other passengers onto Andrei Sakharov Boulevard, I was surprised to see that Mitko knew the area well. Once he had oriented himself, he pointed toward one of the *blokove*, the dire Soviet apartment complexes that line both sides of the boulevard, and said that it was the home of one of his *priyateli*. As was always the case during our time together, I was frustrated by the fragments that were all I could understand of his stories, both because of my poor Bulgarian and because he kept speaking in a kind of code, so that I seldom understood precisely the nature of the relationships he described or why they ended as they did. Never before had I met anyone who combined such transparency (or the semblance of transparency) with such mystery, so that he seemed at once overexposed and hidden behind impervious defenses. We fell silent as we walked toward my building, both of us perhaps thinking of what awaited us there. On my street, the relative prosperity of which marked it off from its neighbors, Mitko turned into a shop for alcohol and cigarettes, a place I stopped at often; the people who worked there knew me, and I wondered uncomfortably what they would think when they saw us together. Mitko walked in first and placed both of his hands palm down on the glass counter, making the shopkeeper wince, and then leaned over to peer at the more expensive bottles displayed on the back wall. He examined several of these, asking the man repeatedly and to his increasing exasperation to pass them over the counter so he could read their labels. He chose the most expensive bottle of gin, as well as a cheap orange soda to accompany it, and then took the bag from my hand to carry it up the three flights to my apartment. I lived in a nice two-bedroom provided by my school, a fact I tried to communicate to Mitko when it became clear he thought I owned it. I don't have that kind of money, I told him, wanting to establish the modest reality of my means, but he greeted the claim with skepticism, even disbelief. But you're American, he said, all Americans have money. I protested, telling him I was a schoolteacher, that I made hardly any money at all; but of course he would think this, having seen my laptop computer, my cell phone, my iPod, signs of comfort if not particularly of wealth in America that here are items of some luxury.

Mitko placed the bag with his bottles on the kitchen counter and opened the cabinets above it, looking for a glass. I stepped up behind him and slid my hands beneath his shirt, pressing my mouth to his neck, but he shrugged me off, saying we had plenty of time for that, he wanted to have a drink first. He took his large tumbler of gin and soda and opened the door to the small balcony that all apartments here have. He stood there for a while as he drank, looking out over the street where I live, which seems never to have been given a name. None of the smaller streets in Mladost have names, though in the center the nation's whole history, its victories and defeats, the many indignities and small prides of a small country, play out in the names of its avenues and squares. Here in Mladost, it's the *blokove*, the huge towers, that anchor one in space, each with its own number individually marked on city maps. As he looked over the street, I asked Mitko what it was he did for a living, by which I meant what it was he had done, before he turned for whatever reason to his *priyateli*. He was smoking a cigarette, that was why he was on the balcony, though as the night wore on this consideration would lapse, and the next morning I would wipe from the floor small piles of gray ash. Largely through gestures, he conveyed that he worked in construction, mimicking with his wounded hands the motions of his trade, going so far as to walk a few steps as he would on a high beam, balancing against the wind. It took me a moment to realize that these movements, which were oddly familiar, were the same as those with which my father, in my childhood, often made us laugh as he told stories about the single summer he spent working construction in Chicago, fresh from his farm in Kentucky, earning his tuition for law school and thus, among other things, purchasing my life.

Mitko told me he was from Varna, a beautiful port city on the Black Sea coast and one of the centers of the astonishing economic boom Bulgaria briefly enjoyed, before, here as in so much of the world, it collapsed suddenly and seemingly without warning. There were some good years, Mitko said, he made good money, and with sudden urgency he dragged me from the balcony toward the table where I had laid my computer. When he opened it, he made a sound of dismay at the state in which I kept it, the screen mottled with dust; *Mrusen*, he said, dirty, with the same tone of voice he would use in response to the requests I made of him later, a tone of mockery and disapproval but also of indulgence, spotting a fault it was in his power either to exploit or to repair. He rose and stepped to the kitchen counter, opening two cupboards and then a third before I understood what he was looking for and fetched the bottle of cleaner from beneath the sink. He put his drink (the large glass almost empty) on the table beside him and placed the computer in his lap, almost cradling it, and with a dampened tissue he began cleaning the screen, not in a desultory hurried way, as I might when finally I bothered, but taking his time, working at it with a thoroughness I would never think it needed. He turned to the keyboard, almost as dirty as the screen, and then he closed the machine and with his fifth or sixth tissue wiped down the aluminum case. *Sega*, he said with satisfaction, now, and set the computer back on its perch, pleased to have done me a service. He opened it again and navigated to a Bulgarian website, an adult social networking site that I knew was popular among gay men. He wanted me to see the pictures from his profile, which he enlarged until they filled the screen. This was two years ago, he said as I looked at the young man in the image, who stood on Vitosha Boulevard with a bag from one of the expensive stores there, smiling radiantly at whoever held the camera, showing his unbroken teeth. I was shocked by the difference between their faces, the man in the image and the man beside me; not only was his tooth unbroken, but also his head was unshaved, his hair full and light brown, conventionally cut. There was nothing rough or threatening about him at all; he looked like a nice kid, a kid I might have had in class at the prestigious school where I teach. It was hardly possible they could be the same person, this prosperous teenager and the man beside me, or that so short a time could have made such a difference, and I found myself looking repeatedly at the screen and then at Mitko, wondering which face was the truer face, and how it had been lost or gained.

Look, Mitko said, pointing as he rattled off the brands of what seemed to me fairly nondescript items of clothing: jeans, a jacket, a button-down shirt; also a belt; also a pair of sunglasses. He even remembered the shoes he was wearing that day, though they weren't visible on the screen; maybe they were special shoes, or maybe it was a special day. *Hubavi*, he said, a word that means lovely or nice, and then, fingering his collar, *mrusen*, and he pulled the offensive shirt off and turned back bare-chested to the screen. I leaned forward (I had sat down next to him) and kissed his shoulder, a chaste kiss, an expression of the sadness I felt for him, perhaps, though it wasn't only sadness that I felt, with his torso now exposed beside me. He looked at me, smiling broadly, the same smile as in the photograph or almost the same, though they looked nothing alike, one transformed—it was astonishing how thoroughly—by the broken tooth, its evidence of something undergone. He bent his head toward mine, but not to engage in the kiss I expected; instead, in a quick surprise, playfully and without any hint of seduction he licked the tip of my nose, then turned back to his task. There were many more photographs, the young man featured in shifting scenes: here at the seaside, here in the mountains, always in the casual clothes of which he was so proud, the generic uniform of affluent young Americans, the stuff of endless racks in endless suburban malls.

Then there were photographs in which he wore nothing at all, angling himself in postures of erotic display that were difficult to reconcile with the sweetly innocent gesture he had just made. In one of these photos Mitko was lying on a bed, leaning on one side so that he faced the camera, fully extending the length of his long body. He was hard, and one of his hands angled his cock, too, toward the lens, the focus and centerpiece of the photograph. He wasn't smiling now, his expression was serious, as is almost always true of the photographs on such sites; I've spent whole nights scrolling through them, feeling an odd mixture of anticipation and dullness, each click a promise of novelty that's never kept. Even without his smile, there was an intensity to Mitko's gaze that convinced me this camera, too, was held by someone significant, someone who elicited his look; and the effectiveness of the photograph (were I scrolling through images I would have lingered, I would have been caught by him) was precisely this gaze, which, though it wasn't meant for any of the men who might be scanning through these pages, still we could claim for ourselves. I tried to claim it now, I turned to Mitko and placed my hand on the inside of his thigh and again leaned in to kiss his neck; the photos had excited me, I wanted to pull him away from the computer. *Chakai*, he said, *imame vreme*, we have time, I want to show you something else. He clicked on another photo, and I saw that I was right, there had been someone behind the camera: a young man of Mitko's height and build, with the same style of hair and dress. They were fully clothed, which only made their embrace more erotic, and their attention was focused wholly on each other; there was no one behind the camera now, it was held by Mitko, one of whose arms extended weirdly toward us, toward me and that other Mitko as we gazed at him together. His other arm was wrapped around the boy, both of whose arms in turn gripped him; they seemed balanced in desire, in their urgency and their hunger for each other. It was tempting to think there was nothing theatrical about this kiss, that it was wholly sincere; and yet the very lens that allowed me access to it made their embrace a pose, so that even if their audience was only hypothetical, even it was only a later version of themselves, later by a year or an hour, still it made their grappling, however passionate, a performance.

Here Mitko, the Mitko who sat next to me, taking long drafts from the tumbler he had refilled, put his finger on the screen, a finger stained with cigarettes (*mrusen*) and flattened with labor, broad and inelegant, the new wounds still fresh at the knuckle. Julien, he said, the man's name, and told me that he was his first *priyatel*, using the word now in a way that was clear, his first boyfriend and, he went on to tell me, his first love. There were more pictures, always the two of them alone, one or the other awkwardly angling the camera. They were so young, these boys in the frame, children really, and yet despite their eagerness for each other it was as though they were documenting something they knew could not last. Of course there were no witnesses in their small town to what they were together, neither their families nor their friends, not even strangers passed on the street, since none of the photos was taken outside. Except for these photographs, these digital memories he scrolled through now, nothing would have survived of those embraces that for all their heat had come to an end. Where is he now, I asked Mitko, flooded with tenderness and wanting access to some greater intimacy with him. He didn't look at me as he answered, still clicking from image to image, his hand moving absently across his chest. He was a schoolteacher, Mitko told me, he left to study abroad and lived in France now, having fled his country along with (I thought) nearly everyone with the talent or means to do so. Of these two men locked together on the screen, then, one left, buoyed by talent or means or both, and the other stayed and was transformed somehow from a prosperous-looking boy to the more or less homeless man I had invited into my home.

As if he sensed my sadness and shared it and wanted to give it voice, Mitko opened a new page, a Bulgarian site for video clips, where one can find almost anything, copyright laws have little meaning here. Music, Mitko said, I want you to hear something, and he typed the name of a French singer, someone I had never heard of and whose name escapes me now, into a search engine that dredged up a remarkable number of files. Mitko scanned through several pages, searching for the clip of a song he had shared with Julien, something they had listened to and loved together. Each of the thumbnail images showed a frail woman softly lit, holding a microphone prayerfully in both of her hands. Maybe all of these clips were from the same concert, or maybe the simple, floor-length white gown she wore in each of them was a sort of signature. Mitko found the video he wanted, and as it began I was moved by the thought that he was granting me access to a private history and so to the intimacy I longed for with him, and that this music, so connected to his past, might allow that intimacy passage across our two languages. And yet, as I watched this woman, who was beautiful with a hollow sort of beauty, I was increasingly repelled by what seemed to me a transparent and entirely artless manipulation. She sang in a choked whisper, affecting an extremity of dignified, photogenic devastation, and at the end of a particularly tragic passage she broke into what seemed to me obviously rehearsed tears, lowering the microphone in a posture of defeat. From time to time, the camera (it was a professional film, an elaborate concert video) positioned itself at the singer's shoulder, forcing us into greater sympathy with her as we shared her vantage on the thousands of fans stretching out into the darkness. They burst into a kind of ecstasy at the sight of her tears, producing collectively a sound of mingled dismay and joy. Ah, said that sound, here at last is the life of significance, the real life that frees us from ourselves.

These thoughts took me away from the moment I shared with Mitko, and made me feel that I too had been played, lured into a sentimentality entirely inappropriate to what was, after all, a transaction. As Mitko continued looking tenderly at the screen, a look that now I suspected was artificial, calculated and sly, I stood up, I put my hands on his shoulders and bent my face once again to his neck. *Haide*, I said, come on, tasting him and tugging at his shoulders. He tried at first to put me off again, he said we could take our time, the night was long; he was counting on a place to spend that night, and no doubt had experienced hospitality withdrawn by men whose desire dissolved immediately to disgust. But I insisted, wanting to assert something, to set the terms of the evening, to claim, finally, the goods for which I had contracted, to put it as brutally as that; it was something brutal that I wanted. When he saw I wouldn't be put off, Mitko became compliant, even eager; he rose from the chair and put his arms around my neck, then hopped and wrapped his legs around me. I had never felt his weight before, he had always been standing when we had sex, and I was surprised by how light he was as I carried him from the kitchen to the bed. I set him down and he stretched out, extending his arms to either side, as if in welcome, and the new sternness I had assumed fell away; I was the compliant one now, this compliance being, finally, what I had purchased. The room was dark, but I could still see him in the light from the hallway and the window, the glow of neon signs and streetlamps, and I gazed at him without moving, as if now that he had given me permission I was hesitant to touch him. He smiled at me, or at what he saw on my face, and then he reached up and pulled me to his mouth, which was sweet with soda. He kept his hand at my neck, and after we kissed he pulled my face away and then pushed my head down; he was already hard, he had responded to our kiss as much as I. But I wasn't so compliant after all, I shook my head to free it, and then I took his hands in mine, as I had imagined doing, his wounded hands, and brought them to my lips. He smiled at me again, tilting his head a little in confusion at the delay, but I didn't delay for long, and he shifted his legs apart as I lowered my mouth to his cock, clasping his hips with both my hands like the brim of a cup from which I drank.

He was wrong to have feared (if he did fear it) that I would want him to leave once he had settled our accounts, as it were, that I would make him return to the center and wander its streets. I wanted him to stay, I wanted to lie close to him, to touch him without passion now but more tenderly, and I felt disappointment and even pain when he bounded up off the bed, as if eager to escape. Everything good, he asked, *vsichko li e nared*, and then he receded down the hall naked, returning to the computer as I put my clothes back on. I heard the sound of more gin being poured, then the pressing of keys, then the distinctive inflating chime of Skype as it opened. I went to join him, and watched as Mitko began what would be a long series of conversations over the Internet, voice and video chats with a number of other young men. I sat in a chair some distance behind him, where I could see the screen without myself falling within the frame. These men seemed all to be speaking from darkened rooms, in voices that were hushed, I realized, to avoid disturbing their families sleeping (it was late now, one or two in the morning) in the next room. Most of them existed only as faces, which was all that could be seen of them in a single bulb's small circle of light. They greeted Mitko fondly, familiarly, though I would come to learn that he had never met most of them in the flesh, that their friendship was restricted to these disembodied encounters. As I listened to these men, all of whom lived outside of Sofia, many in small villages and towns, I was struck by the strangeness of the community they had formed, at once so limited and so lively. Mitko moved from conversation to conversation, speaking and typing at once, the screen lighting up regularly with new invitations. I couldn't follow what they said, I could hardly understand anything; I was exhausted, and as time passed I grew bored. Every now and again I would snap to attention, alerted by some stray word or tone of voice that Mitko was discussing me; and I felt helpless at being the object of conversations I couldn't understand or partake in. Once or twice Mitko orchestrated an introduction, tilting the screen so that I was captured in the image, and the stranger and I would smile awkwardly and wave, having nothing at all to say to each other. I became increasingly ashamed as the night wore on, as more and more I suspected I was the object of mockery or scorn; and besides this I felt bitter at my exclusion from Mitko's enthusiasm, and jealous of the attention he lavished on these other men. To nourish or stave off this bitterness, I'm not sure which, or maybe just out of boredom, I pulled from my shelf a volume of poems and held it open on my lap. It was a slim volume, Cavafy, which I chose in the hope that I would find in it something to redeem my evening, to gild what felt more and more like the sordidness of it. But I was too exhausted to read and flipped the pages idly, afraid that if I went to bed I would wake to find my apartment robbed, that Mitko would take my computer and my phone, things he coveted and that I neglected and (no doubt he felt) didn't deserve. As I turned these pages, failing to find any solace in them, I noticed that the tenor of Mitko's conversations had changed, that he was no longer speaking fondly but suggestively, and that his *priyateli* were now older than he, men in their late thirties or forties. From stray words I caught, it became clear that they were discussing scenarios and prices, that Mitko was arranging his week.

There was one man, older than the others, with whom the conversation was more prolonged. He was heavyset and balding, with a stubbled face that looked at once flabby and drawn in the flat light of the room where he sat smoking one cigarette after another. He lived in Plovdiv, Bulgaria's second-largest city, which escaped bombing in World War II and so retained its beautiful center. As I listened to them speak to each other, listening not to their words but to the tones and cadences of their speech, I remembered the first time I visited this city, the first place I had been outside of Sofia and so my first time seeing the architecture typical of the National Revival, with its elaborate wooden structures and bright pastels that were like expressions of an irrepressible joy, so different from the gray of Mladost. Plovdiv was built, like Rome, as a city of seven hills, which is how many Bulgarians still describe it, though one of the hills was destroyed and mined, in Communist times, for the stones that now pave the streets in the pedestrian center. On one of the remaining hills stands a huge statue of a Soviet soldier, Alyosha he's called by the locals, around whom a large park descends, at each level opening into plazas and observatory points with sweeping vistas of the city. One side of this park is well maintained, with wide staircases and well-kept paths, frequented by couples and families and weekend athletes, society parading its public life. But on my first visit, not knowing any better, a friend and I made our way up the other side of the hill, which seemed largely to have been abandoned. This side too had its stairways and plazas, though the stones shifted and crumbled beneath us; frequently we had to grab at branches or shrubs for balance, once or twice we even dropped to our hands and knees. And yet, as we climbed, it became clear that these paths were not entirely deserted. Pausing to look out at the city and back at the way we had come, we noticed a man on one of the lower observatories whom we hadn't seen on our way up, either because he had been hiding or because we were distracted by our own exertions. He held a plastic bag in one of his hands, which now and again he brought to his face, burying his mouth and nose in it and taking huge, famished breaths; even from a distance we could see the heaving of his shoulders, which shook as if he were weeping. As he lowered the bag from his face his posture softened, his whole frame shrank and relaxed, and he stumbled a little, unsteady on his feet; then he straightened, and advancing to the rusted rail thrust out his arms toward the city, an expression of longing or ecstasy or grief that haunts me still. At one point he gripped this railing with both hands and leaned over it, with great composure vomiting into the bushes below. As we climbed we came across abandoned structures, squat and concrete, slowly being dismantled by incursions of branches and roots, so that often only the outline of a room remained, sometimes only a single wall. But at one observatory point, where again we stopped to catch our breath, there was a line of these structures, concrete shells that, though they lacked doors and windows, seemed otherwise more or less intact. The interiors were too dark to see into, but I had the impression that they extended far back, burrowing into the rock, a network of small cells like a hive or a mine. As we stood there I became aware of three men standing not too far away, who must have hidden at our approach and now emerged from the shadows. They stood apart from one another, solitary figures, middle-aged and lean, each sheltering a cigarette in a cupped palm. Though they never acknowledged our presence or looked our way the air buzzed with an electric charge, and I knew that with a gesture I could have retreated with one of them into those little rooms, as I would have (I was myself humming with it) if I had been alone.

Maybe it was something reminiscent of this charge that caught my attention in Mitko's client or friend, a note of need I hadn't heard in the other men he spoke with. He seemed so eager to please, his eagerness mixed with trepidation; and it seemed to me that Mitko enjoyed the power he wielded, his power to be pleased or to withhold his pleasure. I have something for you, I heard this man say, and heard also *podaruk*, the word Mitko loved and that the man used now for the cell phone he held up to the camera, still in its box, one of the models Mitko had looked at so covetously on Graf Ignatief. And Mitko allowed himself to be pleased, he smiled at the man and thanked him, calling his gift *strahoten*, a word that means awesome and is, like our word, built from a root signifying dread. You have to come

get it, the man said, and Mitko agreed, he would take a bus
to Plovdiv the next day. As I sat there in my fatigue, I realized it was my money that would buy Mitko's ticket to this
man and his expensive gift, and I wondered how it was I
had become one of these men in the dark, offering whatever was asked for something we wouldn't be given freely.
Mitko had already introduced me to the man, he had tilted
the screen toward me so that we could greet each other,
which we did tentatively and with a shade of hostility on
the other man's part, maybe because I was younger than he
and (for a little while yet) more attractive; and maybe simply because I still had possession of Mitko, who told him to
hold up his *podaruk* again, for my admiration or, more likely,
for my instruction. Mitko was still mine for the night, there
were still hours in which he was bound by our phantom
contract; I could still enjoy the desire this man was counting
on as his own, his reward for the extravagance of his gift. I
felt something of the jealousy of ownership, even though my
ownership was temporary, wasn't really ownership at all, and
I was already bitter at the thought of sending Mitko off the
next morning to Plovdiv and this other man, who had lured
him away so easily.

My fatigue was a kind of agitation now, I kept opening
and closing the book I held unread on my lap. I couldn't find
what I had found in it before, the recovery of something
like nobility from the mawkishness of desire, the sense that
stray meetings in dark rooms or the shadowy commerce of
my own evening could burn with genuine luminosity, rubbing up against the realm of the ideal, ready at an instant to
become metaphysics. I set the book aside, seeing that Mitko
was tired too, tired and noticeably drunk; he had emptied
nearly two-thirds of the bottle we had bought. He was unsteady on his feet when he stood up, having said goodbye to

the man in Plovdiv and having announced his intention, finally, to sleep. There were three hours left until we would have to wake, he for his short trip to Plovdiv, a couple of hours on a comfortable bus; and I for a day of teaching, when I would stand before my class wearing a face scrubbed of the eagerness and servility and need it wore as I followed Mitko to the bathroom, standing behind him (he was still naked) as he stood to piss. I rubbed his chest and stomach, lean and taut, the skin of my hands catching just slightly on the bristles of hair; and then, at his words of permission or encouragement, something like Go on, I don't mind, my hands went lower, and gingerly I took the base of his cock and wrapped my hand around the shaft, feeling beneath my fingers the flow of water, heavy and urgent, and feeling too my own urgency, the hardness I pressed against him. He leaned his head back, pressing his face against mine, rubbing it (it too was stubbled and rough) against the softness of my own, and I felt him harden as he finished pissing, as I carefully skinned him back and shook the last of it, feeling almost suffocated with longing, having never touched anyone in that way before, having never before been of that particular service. Mitko turned to me and kissed me, deeply and searchingly and possessively, at the same time pushing me backward down the hallway toward the bedroom, pushing me and perhaps also using me for support, to the broad bed where we had lain together earlier and where now we lay down again. He wrapped his arms around me and pulled me close to him, and not just his arms, he wrapped his legs around me too and with all four of his limbs pressed me to him, embracing me so that when I breathed in the air was filtered through him, smelling of alcohol of course but also of his own scent that elicited such an animal response from me, that so fired me up (I imagined the chambers of the brain lighting up, thrown switches in a house). He lay like some marine creature wrapped around me, wrapping around me again if I shifted or half woke, and I slept as I have seldom slept, deeply and almost without disturbance, held like his beloved or his child; or held, I suppose it must be said, like his captive or his prey.

Not long ago I spent a weekend in Blagoevgrad, in the Pirin mountains, chaperoning a group of students to a conference on mathematical linguistics, a field in which I have little interest and no expertise. I had long hours, while they were in lectures, to explore the beautiful wooded park near our hotel, which followed a small river three kilometers or so toward the pedestrian city center, a haven of humane architecture almost untouched by the ravages of Soviet-era construction, though blemished here and there by gaudy new buildings, expensive apartments overlooking the river. It was spring, the *asmi* were still bare, the wooden trellises built over benches and tables for grapevines to climb, vines that for now were still withered and dry. They clung to their wooden supports, vestiges of winter in a landscape already lush with the turned year. The trees were bright with fresh leaves and with flowers of a sort I had never seen before, blossoms and buds and cones of flowers, a kind of elaborate drunkenness. Our hotel was at the edge of the town, where human habitation made a halfhearted charge farther up the mountains, getting nowhere; just past the hotel's vigorously mowed lawn there were dense woods and thickets and, farther up, dramatic crags. Even in the park

along the river, where I spent my mornings, there was a
kind of romantic wildness to the path between the great
shorn face of the mountain and the river, which, though
small, charged from the peaks with remarkable speed, roar-
ing as it beat against rocks already broken in its bed. As I
walked along that path, I felt drawn from myself, elated,
struck stupidly good for a moment by the extravagant beauty
of the world. The air was thick with movement, butterflies
and day moths and also, hanging iridescent in the sun, tiny
ephemerae shining and embalmed, pushed helplessly here and
there by the light breeze. The grasses and trees were releasing in a great exhalation pods of seeds, the tiny grains each
sheltered and propelled by a tuft of hair like a parachute or
umbrella. I thought, as I watched this sowing of the earth,
of Whitman, whose poems I had just taught to the students
who were listening now to their lectures on mathematical
linguistics, which they would recount to me over dinner
in the town, telling me how they imagined my reactions to
the arguments made about poetry and the structures of meter
and rhyme, their numerical claims on our pleasure. There
were lines in Whitman's poems that had always struck me
as exaggerated in their enthusiasm, their unhinged eroticism;
they embarrassed me a little, though my students loved them,
greeting them each year with laughter. It was these lines that
came to me as I stood on that path in Blagoevgrad, watching
seeds come down like snow, that defined and enriched that
moment. What were those seeds if not the wind's soft-tickling
genitals, the world's procreant urge, and I realized I had always read them poorly, the lines I had failed to understand;
they weren't exaggerated at all, they were exact, and for a
moment I understood his desire to be naked before the world,
his madness, as he says, to be in contact with it. I even felt
something of that desire myself, though it was nothing like
madness for me, in my life lived almost always beneath the

pitch of poetry, a life of inhibition and missed chances, perhaps, but also a bearable life, a life that to some extent I had chosen and continued to choose.

I crossed a small wooden footbridge, stopping briefly to peer at the churning waters and feel their vibration in the structure that held me above them, and found a small café nestled in a bend in the river, on a plot of land the waters had spared. The café was little more than a shack, but clean and well kept; beside it picnic tables were arranged haphazardly by the water. Many of these were taken already, and I had to sit some distance from the river, though I could still hear the water, a sound that has soothed me ever since I was a child. I sipped my cup of coffee and warm milk, looking at the other tables, which were overrun by large, festive groups, and I remembered there was a holiday of some sort that weekend, there are too many here to keep track. Children were playing by the water with balls and sticks and plastic guns emitting light and sound. As I watched them, ignoring the papers I had brought with me to grade, I noticed a younger child, maybe three or four years old, standing apart from the others. She stood at the very edge of the water, and close behind her crouched a man I took to be her father. Again and again, as I watched, this girl, anchored at the waist by the arm of the man behind her, leaned perilously forward (though there was no peril) over the sharp bank, looking down at the water rushing two or three feet beneath her. Repeatedly she leaned forward and repeatedly sprang back, returning to stability with delighted laughter. The fourth or fifth time she did this, she leaned out even farther than before, so that the man had to extend his arm away from his body, almost as far as it would reach. This time she didn't laugh, as if surprised and maybe unnerved by her own audacity, the risk she took in leaning out so far, which of course wasn't a risk at all with her father's arm around her; instead, she threw herself back against her father's body and, reaching her arms up to clasp his neck, pulled his head down (or maybe she didn't have to pull it down), embracing it close to her own. Only then did she laugh, with her father's body folded around her; she laughed with a joy it was difficult for me to recognize, so certain it seemed of a home among the things of the world. They embraced for a long time, a kind of physical contact seldom seen in public, maybe seen only between parents and their very young children, an intimacy confident of absolute possession. Perhaps here, I thought, was a wholly untheatrical embrace. I wasn't the only one moved, I could see others watching them too, smiling and wistful, maybe a little melancholy, as I was, with the sense both of my own exclusion and of how quickly those embraces would pass. They would take on different meanings as the child grew older, they would become impermissible; the same touch that here warmed our hearts would in just a few years elicit our disapproval, our concern, finally our scorn. And so it is, I thought then, as the man and his child released each other and moved away from the water, so it is that at the very moment we come into full consciousness of ourselves what we experience is leave-taking and a loss we seek the rest of our lives to restore. The man and his child returned to their table, the girl running ahead to a woman who bent to lift her into her lap, tickling her a little so that I heard her laugh over the sound of the water. For a moment at least it seemed plausible, the story I told about the sense of dislocation I so often feel, which was eased for the few hours I slept embraced by Mitko, the embrace I returned to in my thoughts as I watched the child and her father by the river in Blagoevgrad.

That morning I spent grading papers was almost two months after my final meeting with Mitko in Varna, a meeting that was itself preceded by three months of silence. In the

days and weeks that followed the night we spent together
in Mladost, one of only two nights, as it turned out, we
would spend together in all the months we knew each other,
Mitko appeared at my apartment every few days, always
friendly and eager, and always with some request. Whenever I heard the ringing of the bell linked to the street entrance, which no one else ever rang, I felt torn between a
desire on the one hand for the routines of solitude (my
writing and my books); and, on the other, for the thrill of
Mitko's presence and its disruption of all routine. But after
weeks of these visits I'd had enough disruption, and I came
to resent the requests he made, which were never exorbitant
(money for cigarettes or credit for his phone, once forty leva
for a pair of shoes), but which it seemed would never end.
Still, on the very evening I put a stop to these visits, my heart
leapt up as it always did at the buzzer's announcement of
his presence. He was friendly when I opened the door and
seemed well enough, but I was worried by the state of him;
his clothes, about which he was usually so fastidious, were
dirty, and as he walked past me I could smell it had been
days since he had bathed. We had just sat down on the couch,
he had just smiled at me in invitation and I had laid my
head on his chest, inhaling his sour smell, when there was a
knock at the door. I had forgotten about my dinner with C.,
a friend who lived on the floor above me and also taught at
the American College; he had come to pick me up on the
way to a restaurant nearby. Mitko was delighted to see this
friend, whom he had met before on one of his visits and
with whom he was clearly smitten, as was nearly everyone
who met C., who had an effortless, ingratiating charm and
was nonetheless entirely indifferent to the needs and desires
of others, so that he seemed always to be receding while
still inviting pursuit. Mitko hardly took his eyes off him
and touched him whenever he could, always robust and

friendly touches, a physical language he used to compensate
for their inability to speak to each other; and yet touches that,
though there was nothing at all seductive about them, I knew
would at the slightest sign of permission or desire have taken
on a sexual heat.

At dinner, Mitko ordered far more than he could consume, as he always did, food and drink and cigarettes. I was
soon exhausted by my attempts to translate, and we settled
into a silence interrupted by Mitko's sallies at conversation,
nearly all of them directed, through me, to C. Maybe it was
out of jealousy, then, that I suddenly asked Mitko whether
he liked his life among his *priyateli*, putting the question as
baldly as that. *Ne*, he answered with the same bluntness, showing his usual reticence to discuss anything unpleasant, especially about his past or how he had reached his present. I
pressed him, unsure whether I was motivated by cruelty or
interest or concern, and, entirely neglecting my friend, who
was unable to follow even my halting Bulgarian, I asked
Mitko why then he chose to live as he did. I knew the question was naïve, or not even that; it was unfair, it presumed a
freedom of choice that implied a judgment I had no business making. *Sudba*, Mitko said, fate, the single word serving
to dismiss at a stroke all choice and consequence. In Varna
there were no jobs, he said, and in Sofia what jobs there were
were shut off to him, since he had no address he could give
to employers, and no way to get an address without work.
This was the end of our exchange, which colored the re-
mainder of the evening, for the rest of which there would
be no more innuendo from Mitko (innuendo that I had
received ambivalently, to his visible confusion) and during
which in other respects as well his mood was subdued, as
was my own. At one and the same time, I wanted to repair
the damage I had done and sensed with relief the possibility
of extricating myself from an entanglement that had be-

come more intricate than I could bear. It seemed to me
there was no attitude toward Mitko I could take that would
let me be at once sufficiently compassionate and sufficiently
free, so that I wavered between eagerness and distance, an
ambivalence that I knew, though it was especially acute with
Mitko, characterized all of my relationships, casual and pro-
found. When we stood up from the table, I told Mitko I
would walk with him to the metro, making clear that this
once, at least, we wouldn't be having sex. I was relieved to
make this clear, to find I was able to make it clear, but I still
didn't feel at ease with myself or with him, and the mood
was heavy as we walked. I had asked C. to come too; I
thought he would help my resolve, and I didn't want to be
alone when I saw Mitko off, but he kept his distance, walking a few steps behind us. Finally I asked Mitko if he was all
right, unable to bear his silence anymore. He looked away
from me, toward the traffic on the boulevard, and said *Iskam
da zhiveya normalno*, I want to live a normal life. I was silent
for a moment, torn between a terrible sadness and my desire
for escape. And then, watching his face, I don't want to be one
of your clients, I said. He turned to me in surprise, saying
But you aren't a client, you're a friend, but I waved this ob-
jection away. I like you too much, I said, clumsily but with
candor, it isn't good for me to like you so much. We had
reached the station by then, and he stood a moment looking
at me with bemusement, not quite sure what to make of what
I had said, and perhaps wondering which of the faces I had
shown him was the true face, the face of need he had been
accustomed to, or this new face that suddenly was closed to
him. Then, as if deciding it wasn't worth his while to understand, he shrugged and put out his hand, asking for a ten-leva
note to see him on his way.

For three months there was no sign of Mitko, and over the course of that time my surprise that he would take my parting words to him seriously turned to concern and finally, inevitably, to longing. It was on a weekend afternoon late in February that with a ping he appeared on Skype, from which he had been absent all that time, as he had been absent from NDK and from the streets I had begun to haunt in the hope of finding him again and of picking up the thread I had (as it seemed to me now) too quickly and with too little thought let drop. How extraordinary that with the press of a key, allowing no time for regret, my screen should be filled with his moving image, dear to me again after the long absence. He was peering at his own screen, his face, at first knit with attention, suddenly relaxing and coming alive, as he smiled with what seemed a genuine smile at seeing me after all this time. As we spoke, I stared at his image as if to consume it, taking in what I was surprised to find I had nearly forgotten, though he had let me take photographs of him that night we spent in my apartment, dozens of them, and I had looked at them often in the months he had been gone. But now I could see how he moved, the gestures he made that were too swift for photographs, the living tale of him, and I was filled with a longing free of all ambivalence. He looked better than the last time I had seen him, his clothes were clean, his head freshly shaved, so it was a shock to learn that he had spent the last ten or so weeks in a hospital in Varna, laid up with a liver disorder of some kind. I couldn't make out the details, either because of my Bulgarian or because he shied away from telling me too much. He did speak of the terrible boredom he felt in the hospital, where he was confined to a bed, without a computer or even a television for distraction, since the one mounted in his room would only play if fed constantly with coins. Nor were books or magazines a diversion, since he read Cyrillic with difficulty; he had left school in the seventh grade, and was more comfortable with the Latin characters used in Internet chat rooms. He confessed this to me with evident shame one day when I had run out briefly for something he wanted—cigarettes or alcohol or the sweets he loved—and returned to find him at the computer moaning with frustration, unable either to type in the Cyrillic script it was set to or to switch it back. His only visitors had been his mother and grandmother and the boy he called *brat mi*, whom I hadn't seen since that first day at NDK.

But he was better now, he said, he felt fine, though in a month he was supposed to return to the hospital, for a stay that might be as long as the first. I thought of how often, for all his ebullience, I had seen Mitko sick, his colds, the ear infection he had had for weeks, the herpes that sometimes disfigured his mouth; I thought of his drinking and the risks of his trade, and for an instant I wanted desperately to save him, though from what exactly and how I wasn't sure. I knew it was a ridiculous desire, that it imagined a relationship I didn't want; and I also knew Mitko had never expressed any desire of his own to be saved. He was in an Internet café (every now and again I saw someone walk by behind him), and he made more and more use of the keyboard as we talked, typing comments that were too suggestive for him to speak out loud. This had the effect he intended, overwhelmingly when he stood and under the pretext of stretching displayed his body to me, reaching into his pockets to pull the folds of his jeans tight against his crotch. By the end of the conversation, surprising myself, I had proposed to come to Varna at the end of the week, a proposition he was eager to accept. I will be with you the whole weekend, he said, I promise, *hundert protzent*.

Over the next few days I received a number of e-mails from him, as he visited hotels and reported back on prices and their nearness to the sea. It was the sea, as the days passed, that I longed for almost as much as I longed for Mitko, having spent so many months in landlocked Sofia, and it was the thought of the sea even more than of Mitko that I dwelled on for the seven cramped hours I spent on the bus from Sofia to the coast. It was a gray day, cold, more like winter than spring. There were *martenitsi* pinned to everyone's clothes, small bundles of red and white yarn exchanged on the first of March, a ritual meant to encourage the year to turn. My own bag was covered with them; students had given them to me with great ceremony, with wishes of health and wealth and happiness, all day long. But there was no magic in them, and for the whole trip a light precipitation fell, sometimes as rain, sometimes as snow. I was depressed by both the weather and the landscape we passed, the beauty of which was ruined everywhere human hands had touched it. Along the highway, which must have dated to Communist times, the buildings we passed were squat and concrete and often falling apart, abandoned no doubt for their larger counterparts in the city I had just left. I was amazed by how completely the impulse to beauty had been erased from these buildings, which were so different, in everything but their poverty, from the mountain villages I had visited, where almost every dwelling showed as if defiantly an urge toward art.

As evening fell, the landscape darkened and was lost, and the window offered nothing but the reflection of my own face. I've never been able to read on buses, and so the only distraction from the discomfort of the ride was the line of small screens that ran the length of the center aisle, looping the same low-budget American action movie over and over. There was no sound, and the subtitles moved too quickly for me to puzzle them out, but even so I was unable to stop watching. It was a terrible movie, a revenge tragedy, every shot was a cliché. In each scene the violence grew more brutal, the tortures more baroque, my own excitement more intense; and not just my own, at one point I heard a woman gasp and glanced away from the screen and saw that nearly everyone on the bus was transfixed. The film had bound us together, it had made us all feel the same thing, so that we became a kind of temporary corporate body. How easily we are made to feel, I thought, and with what little foundation, with no foundation at all. At the movie's climax, a final scene of slaughter and settling of accounts, an old man across the aisle breathed *Chestito*, well done, just loudly enough to be heard, and it was almost as if I had spoken the word myself.

As we neared Varna, the lights of the city drew me back to the windows, to the blurred world glimpsed through glass streaked with rain. We stopped at the edge of the city center, or what I took to be the city center, not at a terminal but in a lot beside a gas station, where Mitko was standing without an umbrella, his shoulders hunched against the rain. I was the first off the bus, bounding out to greet him, so overcome with excitement that he had to send me back for my bag, which I had left on the seat beside me. We both laughed at this, at my eagerness and forgetfulness, and he shook his head in rebuke and indulgence, having provided once again a service beyond the terms of our contract. He took the bag from me, insisting with a show of gallantry when I said I could carry it myself, and led me to a line of taxis. He asked me about the trip, if I was hungry, if I wanted to go straight to the hotel or explore a bit first, though of course he already knew my answer to these questions. It was a short drive to the hotel he had chosen, a nice place, he said, very close to the sea. And it was nice, in a faded way, two old houses around a courtyard on a narrow street off the city's main square, the pedestrian avenue leading to the sea. There was a single attendant, an old man who came out of his booth, a glassed-in porch attached to one of the buildings, to greet us. He and Mitko shook hands warmly, and I wondered what their relationship was, whether Mitko came here often with men, whether perhaps they had some arrangement. Our room was shabby and spacious, on the first floor with large windows that faced the street and were inadequate against the wind. There was a stand-alone radiator against one of the walls, and Mitko went over to it and switched it on; he must have been chilled to the bone from his wait. He sat on top of it, sighing with pleasure as it warmed. Without getting up, he reached to the old television against the wall and flipped through the few channels, stopping at a station playing videos of Balkan pop-folk songs; he hummed along, wagging his head from side to side with the jagged rhythms as he fiddled with my iPod, which I had set on the bedside table when we arrived and which he immediately snatched up. It took him a moment to realize it wasn't the same device that had so fascinated him in Sofia, and when I told him that that one had been stolen, that a man had taken it from me during an encounter, he shook his head in sympathy—such is the world—and then his features hardened. When I'm in Sofia, he said, we'll look for him, you show me who he is and I'll take care of him. *Samo da go vidya i do tam.* It was clear that his sickness, whatever it was, hadn't kept him from the brawls I suspected he enjoyed; above his left eye, now, there was a wound just a day or two old, the skin still split. I tried to delay, settling in a bit, arranging my things, but his presence was too much for me, I went to him and touched him and he put his hand on my neck and pushed me down, then unbuttoned his fly and fished himself out, still clutching my iPod in his other hand. It was only when I stood up again and took his arm, tugging him toward the bed, that he laid the device aside and made himself more fully available to me. But he was still detached, he kept glancing at the television, and when I asked him what was wrong he just shrugged and answered that he had already had sex that afternoon, which seemed like a breach of contract, though I suppose I had no real basis for complaint. I fell back from him then, I lay next to him thinking, as I had had cause to think before, of how helpless desire is outside its little theater of heat, how ridiculous it becomes the moment it isn't welcomed, even if that welcome is contrived. Mitko was right next to me, naked now and stretched out with his arms behind his head, but he didn't touch me or respond to my touch, his cock lay half-hard against his stomach. He was granting me access but he wasn't really present, and finally I fell back beside him, my eyes closed, and concentrated on his warmth where our bodies touched as I brought myself off.

I woke early the next morning and went for a walk on my own. The sun was just rising, the wind was chill and fresh and laced with salt. Mitko had told me that the hotel was close to the sea, and as I turned from our street into the main plaza, I gasped at the horizon of water framed grandly by the pillars at the entrance of the Sea Garden. I quickly got lost in this large park, wandering paths that seemed to lead toward the water only to veer away. I loved the silence of the morning, and also the solitude that seemed part of the design of the place, or rather the rhythm it established of solitude and conviviality, the narrow, wooded paths giving out suddenly onto plazas with benches gathered at observatory points over the sea, which was endless and gray and pierced ceaselessly by gulls. After the desolation of the landscape I had seen the day before, I was moved to be in a place designed so clearly with beauty in mind. The very layout of the paths, with their apparent aimlessness, seemed to rebuke the bare utility of the buildings we had passed on the bus. The park was built shortly after liberation, and as I wandered I came upon statues of revolutionaries and writers placed here and there along the paths. Some of their names were familiar to me, but not many of their stories, so that it was like walking a peculiarly lyrical account of the past, free of the usual narratives of triumph and loss. There were signs, too, in the darkest and most overgrown eddies, of the park's other life, secret and ludic: cigarette butts and bottles and the occasional distended dry husk of a condom. They must have been left there the previous summer, when these paths would have been a carnival, filled with vacationers from across Europe, the beautiful young fueled by night and heat and the ever-present sea.

It was the sea I longed for now, after so much misdirection and delay. Again and again the staircases I encountered leading down from the garden's observatories to the beach were cordoned off, in such crumbling disrepair as to prevent safe passage. I was aware of time passing and knew I should get back to the hotel, to Mitko who might be waking to find me gone. When I finally made my way down from the garden, I was frustrated to find that access to the water was blocked by a seemingly endless line of construction, complexes of restaurants and casinos and discotheques, all of them boarded up for the season, barricaded against sea and weather and, I assumed, the plundering hands that had covered these boards with graffiti. And yet, when I did find a way through these linked complexes, reaching not quite the beach yet but the road that ran alongside it, I turned away after only a few moments. The wind coming off the sea, unbroken by trees or by the buildings that had frustrated my approach, was too fierce to stand facing it for long. And I was fascinated by those buildings, now that I saw the other side of them, with their garish, amusement-park facades rising above their boarded windows. I could hear a radio playing faintly from within one of the restaurants, but there was no other sign of human presence, no voices or movement save for the cats that had improvised some habitation on the rooftops, where they watched me, disinterested and alert. There was a ghostliness about the whole strip, as if it had been abandoned for years. One restaurant wasn't boarded up, I don't know why, and I walked up the few steps to the deck to peer in through the glass, which was crusted with salt and sand. It was a place for children, a restaurant and playroom both, with figurines and coin-operated rides in the shapes of characters from American cartoons. These were wrapped in sheets of plastic, further blurring an image already blurred by the glass, so that they were grotesquely distorted; and for a moment, as I looked at these figures I associated with my childhood, it was as if they took on a kind of agonized life, like quarantined victims of some plague or like infants themselves, suffocating in plastic cauls.

Mitko was awake when I returned to the hotel, lounging and watching television, unperturbed by my absence, though he wanted to know where I had been and took my camera to scan through the photos I had taken. He knew every inch of the park, he said, he recognized each of the scenes on the screen, and he demonstrated this knowledge by describing for me what lay outside the frame. Later that afternoon he took me into the center, through its streets and squares, pointing out landmarks that were like miniatures of their counterparts in the capital: monuments to the same patriots, museums of history, of archaeology and ethnography, the Roman ruins and the central cathedral with its efflorescence of domes. Everywhere there were gulls, tame and inquisitive as cats, filling the squares with their cries. Mitko was hungry, and we stopped at a snack stand, a bakery selling cheese pastries and sausages and sweets of various kinds. We stood in the street to eat, a small pedestrian square lined on one side by the opera house, and soon we were accosted by one of these birds, who trotted intently before us, working the hinges of its bill and raising its wings as it cried. Mitko had ordered more food than he could eat, and he threw one of his scraps to this bird, which beat its wings to catch it in midair, tossing it back quickly and repeating its demands. Soon there were four or five of them hopping and calling, so that the air was full of opening doors. They delighted me, and Mitko fed my delight as he fed the birds, to the last scrap, after which he raised his hands in apology for having nothing left. As we continued our walk, Mitko told me stories about the places we passed, here the restaurant he frequented with Julien, here the scene of a nocturnal encounter, here the table outside of a *dyuner* stand where, drunk and brawling, he fell and struck his mouth, breaking his tooth. When it was dark, he said, he would take me to the thermal baths, pools where despite the cold we could lounge in the water together. And he wanted me to see his home, he said; the next morning we would take the bus to the *blokove* on the outskirts and I would meet his mother and his grandmother. I was surprised by this; I suppose he wanted to show me off, a foreigner, a teacher at a famous school, though how he would explain our acquaintance I had no idea.

Everywhere we went he greeted people by name, shaking their hands, patting their backs like a politician, an unaccountably public man. He gestured toward me in introduction, saying that I was his friend, an American, at which point I nodded politely and waited for the conversation to end. As we walked away from certain of these men, Mitko would lean into me and whisper a suggestion that we might all three have fun together, he could easily arrange it. But I wanted to be alone with Mitko, and I told him this later, back in the room when he suggested he call his friend, the one he called *brat mi*, who was, he assured me, as eager as Mitko himself for the three of us to meet. We would gather at the hotel, he said, and then go to the hot springs together. It was already early evening, night was falling, he said we could leave soon. But I want to be with you, I said, only with you, and he smiled and allowed himself to be dragged to the bed, where I tugged off his shoes, unbuttoned his pants and his shirt. He lay next to me, accepting my caresses, every now and then propping himself up to drink from the whiskey he had poured himself as soon as we got in, despite his illness and his pledge, he had told me, to drink less. He was watching television as well, flipping through channels until he stopped at a film, an American film dubbed in Bulgarian, as though to distract himself from what I was doing to him, so that I felt not only alone in my longing, but for the first time like an aggressor. When I pulled back from him, he reached down and started to stroke himself, slowly and with something like languor, even when he went soft maintaining the same regular motion of his arm.

It was now, lying next to him but excluded from this mechanical exercise, that I noticed the movie he had chosen. It was a famous film, recent, a historical drama that for all its artifice was as brutal as the film I had watched on the bus the day before. But this was a different sort of violence, more invested in genuine suffering; it wasn't gunfire and explosions we watched, Mitko and I, but the lashing of whips and the hacking of swords. It killed my desire, but Mitko watched it without once looking away, not avidly but with a strange dullness, the same quality with which his hand moved at his waist. Can we change it, I said, can we watch something else, but he murmured no, he was watching, it was interesting, he wanted to see what would happen. It was history I had learned in school, first as a child and then again later, when I could understand more of its horror; I knew what would happen, and I didn't want to be drawn into that cumulative helplessness portrayed on the screen. I wanted him to stop jerking off to these images, though it didn't seem to me that that was quite what he was doing, the two actions—his eyes motionless and his hand in constant motion—seemed detached from each other, even if they shared the same languorous quality. Maybe you want to stop, I said, you don't have to finish now, using the Bulgarian euphemism *svurshish*, more accurate but less hopeful than our own verb, come, the openness of which I preferred, you can wait until later. But he didn't want to wait, he said he was close, though he wasn't close, there was still no urgency in his movement, no variation of tempo at all. I lay there for another quarter hour, watching him and watching the images on the screen, feeling an acidic sense of entrapment. He did finally finish, and it was only then that he touched me, at the last moment he reached out and pulled my head to him and filled my mouth, which felt less like an erotic act than a convenience, a way quite simply of cleaning up. And now his languor disappeared, he seemed pleased with himself, filled with ebullient energy. The third time today, he said, switching off the television as he turned to me and grinned, and then explained, seeing my confusion, that he had jerked off twice that morning while I was exploring the Sea Garden. What do you mean, I said, surprised, though as I spoke my surprise was changing to something else, and a note in what I said put Mitko on his guard. What, he said, lifting himself from the bed to the chair beside it and reaching for the pack of cigarettes he had already emptied, which he crumpled in annoyance and then tossed aside. He reached instead for his drink, though it too was empty and he had to pour himself another from the bottle on the floor. Are you mad at me, he asked, and I wasn't quite, anger wasn't really what I felt, or not yet. Why would you do that, I said, why would you do that alone when you know how much I want it? I couldn't do any better than that, I had to speak baldly in his language, without any of my usual defenses. But you weren't here, Mitko said, I woke up and you were gone, I didn't know where you were or when you would be back, why should I wait—and here he smiled and held up his hands, trying to lighten the tone—I'm a young guy, I can't wait, I don't have that much control.

I didn't respond to his smile. I came all the way from Sofia, I said, and I've paid for the room, for our meals, for everything, I came to be with you, to have sex with you— and here Mitko broke in, catching the scent of something he could exploit. Is it just about sex then, he said, you're my friend, and he used again that word *priyatel*. I found the hotel, he said, I waited for you at the bus stop, even though it was raining, and now my throat hurts, I'm starting to get sick. *A ne e li vyarno*, he said, isn't that right, challenging me to deny it. He paused to drink, as though bracing himself for a confrontation he knew he couldn't avoid. I did all that because we're friends, he said, those are things friends do, it isn't just sex for me. He stopped then, as if he realized he had gone too far, had leaned too hard on the fiction of our relationship and felt the false surface give way. But we aren't friends like that, I said as Mitko took another long drink.

We both get something from it, I went on, and the bluntness of the language was now the tool I wanted: I get sex, I
said, and you get money, that's all. But now I was the one
who had gone too far, and so I softened what I had said, or
tried to: I like you, I said, I like being with you, *skup si mi*, I
said, you're dear to me, you're beautiful. But Mitko's expression had hardened. He set down his glass and placed
both of his hands on his knees. When have I ever said no to
you, he asked, and it was true, though he had delayed and
put me off he had always given in when I insisted, he had
never truly refused. The trouble with you is you don't know
what you want, he said, you say one thing and then another.
I knew he was right, and not just about my relationship
with him; always I feel an ambivalence that spurs me first in
one direction and then another, a habit that has done much
damage. I didn't deny what he said, I even nodded in agreement, at which his mood only darkened. I'm not like that,
he went on, I'm a man of my word, if I say that I'm through
with you I'm through, I won't change my mind, and if I see
you again, if we pass each other in the street, at NDK, in
Plovdiv, in Varna, it doesn't matter where, I'll pretend I don't
know you, he said, I won't even say hello. Is that what you
want, he said, and then, without pausing for me to respond,
be careful. There wasn't anything playful or warm about him
now; though he sat naked in front of me he was entirely un-
available. Be sure you tell the truth, he said, be sure you say
what you mean. But how could I say what I meant, I thought,
when that meaning so entirely escaped me?

  I looked at him without speaking, at the length of him
folded in the chair; it was a way of delaying an answer but it
was also a valedictory look, I was taking him in with a sense
already of regret. He saw me looking as he poured himself
another drink, his third or fourth in a short time, the effects
of it were beginning to show; and again I had the thought,

more troubling now, that he was steeling himself for something to come. Well, he said, which is it, and though I hadn't
come any closer to a decision I felt pressed to meet his tone,
a pressure I was grateful for, since it freed me from having to
choose. Yes, I said then, yes, I think that's best, but I didn't
stop there; I'm sorry, I said, I'm sorry, and then, this is sad
for me, *tuzhno mi e*. He looked at me silently, then stood up
and began pulling on his clothes, moving purposefully but
also unsteadily. Think if I were someone else, he said, and
there was tension in his voice, he was speaking more quickly
and I had to strain to understand him, think if I were a
different person, if I were like that guy who stole from you,
have you thought about that? Did you think about that
when you took me home with you? He looked different to
me now as he stared at me again, he wore a face I hadn't seen
before, a face that grew stranger and unsettled me more as
he went on. I could have been anyone, I could have robbed
you, I could have taken your camera and your phone, your
computer, I could have hurt you. Did you think about that,
he asked again, and he paused, he looked at me with his new
face, which was capable, it seemed to me, of any of those
things, and I wondered whether it was a face he had just
discovered or one he had hidden all along.

I stood up, feeling the need to assert my presence, and
also to place myself between him and the pile of my be-
longings I had gathered in one corner; I felt threatened by
him, which was what he intended me to feel. At first it was
as though this had its effect, he seemed to beat a kind of
retreat. But I'm not that sort of person, he said, though this
wasn't a retreat at all, it was just the start of a new theme. If
it weren't for me you wouldn't even have them, he went on,
stepping up to me where I stood, nobody needed to steal
them, you left it all on the bus, and again he gave an inventory of what I owned, what I had brought with me that

might fetch him a few hundred leva in the pawnshops of Varna. *Ne e li vyarno*, he said again, working himself up, if it weren't for me you would have lost them anyway, you owe me, and he punctuated this last with a touch, not quite adversarial yet but assertive, putting his hand on my shoulder and pushing to see how far I would give way. All the while he held his face close to my own, his new face, and I felt the beginning of fear like a light current, a prickling along the nerves. Mitko, I said, softly but I hoped with confidence, saying his name again as if to call back the face I knew, Mitko, you should leave now, it's time for you to leave. He smiled at this, he widened his eyes with amusement and took a half step away, Is it time for me to leave, he said, quoting my words back to me, is it? And he turned a little and made a sound, *hunh*, a sound of puzzlement and continued amusement, not an angry sound, and when he turned back his arm swung in a wide arc and he struck me, with the back of his hand he struck my face, only once and not very hard, so that when I fell back upon the bed it was as much from the shock as from the force of it, from shock and from the passivity that has always been my instinctive response to violence. We both froze then, I on the bed and he standing in front of it, as if both of us were waiting to see what would happen next. I felt real fear now, physical and immediate and, strangely enough, already fear of the more distant future, as I wondered how badly I would be bruised and how I would explain it to my students. I watched Mitko, and it seemed to me he was surprised by what he had done, that maybe he was frightened too by what he might do next. He only stood there an instant before he propelled himself forward and fell on top of me, and I must have flinched, I must have shut my eyes, though it wasn't a blow I felt on my face but his mouth, his tongue as it sought my own mouth, which I opened without thinking. I let him kiss me though it didn't seem like a kiss, his tongue in my mouth, it was an expression not of tenderness or desire but of violence, as was the weight with which he bore down on me, pinning me to the bed as he ground his chest and then his crotch against me; and then he grabbed my own crotch with one hand, gripping it not painfully but commandingly, and I thought whatever happens next I will let it happen. But nothing happened next, he was on me, unbearably present, and then he sprang off the bed and was gone, without taking anything or speaking another word, though of course he could have taken whatever he wanted.

I lay there after he left, feeling my fear, which grew more intense, so that for a minute or perhaps for two or three I couldn't force myself to move, not even to close the door. I observed, as if at a distance, my quick breathing and the pain I felt, not an especially bad pain, maybe there would be no bruise to explain away. Finally I hauled myself up, surprised by how unsteady I was though so little had happened, everything was fine, I said to myself, I was safe now. But as I turned the latch on the door I realized I wasn't safe, that the thin tongue of metal between the two wooden wings might easily be forced, it offered almost no resistance at all. And the latches on the windows were flimsy too, a push would be enough to snap them. They were large windows, big enough to pass in or out of, and some of them faced the street, which meant there wouldn't be any need to enter the courtyard to gain access, anyone could avoid the supposed watchman sleeping in his glassed-in porch. I paused then and looked at those windows, realizing that I was visible to anyone peering in through the ill-fitting drapes. So the crisis isn't past, I thought, using that word, crisis; I was right to still be afraid. I was frozen in place, pinned where I stood, a feeling I remembered from childhood, when stillness was the only response to the terror I often felt at night. It was all

I could do to reach out and turn off the lights, listening for any noise outside as I thought again of the face Mitko had shown me, his real face, I thought now. He had so carefully arranged our trip; maybe he had chosen this hotel not because of price or its nearness to the sea, but for a different set of reasons altogether, its ease of access and the inadequacy of its locks. I thought of the many friends he had introduced me to, some of whom he had encouraged me to invite into our room, where I would have been, it now occurred to me, completely vulnerable; I thought of the boy he called *brat mi*, who had been so obedient in the bathrooms at NDK, ready to do Mitko any service. They were probably together at that very moment, walking the streets as Mitko waited for the right time to come back. All of Mitko's proposals seemed to me now like snares, the invitation to the thermal baths, even to his home among the *blokove*, both of them places where Mitko might have become any of the hypothetical selves he had listed, might have become all of them at once.

I was convinced now, there would be no sleep for me in that room, and so I gathered together my things and went out into the central yard. The attendant emerged from his booth to meet me; he was the same man who had greeted Mitko so warmly the night before, and surely he had seen him leave. He was full of solicitude when I told him I wanted to change my room, though he did ask me why; *Ne mi e udobno*, I said, unable to say more, it isn't comfortable for me. He shrugged at this and smiled, and then showed me to a much smaller room with a single window that faced the courtyard, looking almost directly at the attendant's porch. He helped me transfer my things, made sure I was satisfied, and then looked at me expectantly, as if knowing I must have more to say. The man who was with me, I said then, burning with shame to say it, he shouldn't come back here, he isn't welcome, he's not my friend. At this the man's face brightened, not with malice or the scorn I had feared, but with comprehension, and also with a sympathy I hadn't expected. I understand completely, he said, don't worry about anything, I'll watch for him and if he shows up here I'll make sure he won't bother you. He was briefly silent, and then, It's a shame there are such people in the world, he said, you have to be so careful, you pay them, you have your fun, and then they should leave—but sometimes they don't leave, they want more than you agreed. It's a shame, he repeated after a pause in which it was clear I had nothing to add; I was paralyzed with humiliation and wanted only for him to go. But don't worry, he said as he opened the door, this is a good room—and here he reached over to arrange the curtains so that the glass was more fully covered—you're safe here, don't worry. Then he was gone, finally, and I locked the door behind him and lay down on the bed, feeling relief now but also the anger of having been subjected to something, an anger like the dry grinding of gears. Maybe it was an anger that Mitko knew well, I thought suddenly, that he knew better than I. I closed my eyes as I lay there, though it would be a long time before I slept.

I woke early the next morning. There was an eerie quality to the light seeping in around the drapes, and when I pulled them aside I saw that the air was full of snow, though the flakes were fine and not yet sticking to the ground. In the bathroom I studied my face, tilting it back and forth in the light, relieved that I could hardly see a bruise. I stepped out of my room, giving a wave to the watchman, who must have been coming to the end of his shift, and turned toward the Sea Garden, wanting to see the water again. The park wasn't deserted this time, despite the hour and the snow; as I walked I passed old couples strolling briskly, men with their dogs, even cyclists, all out for a morning's exercise be-

side the sea. Just past the entrance on the left there was a
huge casino complex, from the depths of which I could hear
the driving beat of dance music; there must have been a
disco there, where even in the off-season the morning had
yet to come. I wanted to see the water, but not just to see
it; I wanted to be close to it, to imagine if not to feel the
unearthly cold of it. And so I walked more purposefully
through the garden, bypassing, as best I could, its more
winding paths, and when I reached again the line of hotels
and bars and, beyond them, the road, I didn't retreat, I crossed
the road and held my face to the wind, though it was biting
and filled now with snow. Three long walkways extended
from the beach into the sea, branching out at their ends into
three separate promenades, like the arms, it seemed to me,
of a snowflake as drawn by a child. I walked to one of these
piers, which unlike the park was deserted, as was the sea,
except for the gulls and, far out in the water, two huge
tankers that sat unmoving at the horizon. At the near end of
the pier there was a large stone sculpture, two stylized figures in robes, who might as easily have been monks as sailors
and who seemed to be embracing although they were looking away from each other, one toward the sea and one
toward the shore, an image of irreconcilable desires. The stone
was pocked and scarred, already dissolving in the abrasive
air. I walked the length of the pier, which was lined with
huge stone objects shaped like jacks from the children's game,
a defense against the heavier element of the sea. I walked to
the farthest point of the pier, to its very edge, and spent some
time looking at these stones and at the white froth surging
between them. I felt the pressure of the water striking the
stones and the steadfastness of their resistance, of what seems
like their resistance and is simply a slower giving way. The
snow was easing now though the wind was still fierce, the air
tossed the birds as wildly as the sea. I could already sense

remorse gathering, it was distant and abstract still but I knew it would flood in, that it would be terrible, and as I watched the motion of the sea I accused myself, thinking bitterly oh, what have I done. I stood there until I was chilled beneath my clothes and my face was numb with cold. Then I turned and walked back toward the shore, stamping my feet a little to quicken the sluggish blood.

II

A GRAVE

I was in the middle of a sentence when there was a knock
at the door and a woman entered my classroom without a
word. I knew her, of course, she worked in the front office
of my school, but there was something in her manner that
checked my greeting before I spoke it, perhaps her silence
or the oddly formal way she carried the single, unfolded
page in her hand, so that she walked toward me through an
atmosphere strangely ruffled or unquiet, in which my interrupted sentence still hung. The students perked up at her
knock, not that they had been to that point bored exactly,
but any interruption is welcome, and especially when it
suggests some hidden drama, as when this woman, whom I
considered almost a friend, who had always been kind to me
and who surely thought she was doing me a kindness now,
walked quickly but with a subdued manner to deliver me
what she held. I found myself flustered as I took the page
from her hand, standing awkward in front of students to
whom a moment before I had been speaking freely, even
eloquently, rehearsing thoughts that had burned for me once
and that now were a repertoire of dull gestures, a custom.
It was mid-September, the very beginning of the year; the
sun beat down and the room, which was high and received

the brunt of the morning light, was almost unbearably hot, despite the windows we had opened. It was toward these windows that I longed to look, not toward the page now in my hand but toward the trees and the field beyond them and the road and, though I had only a glimpse of it, the mountain that hovered beyond the huge blocks of government buildings. But of course I did look at the page, an e-mail that had been sent to the school's address and that this woman, my friend or almost friend, had printed out to deliver by hand. She stood beside me as I read, still without speaking, and her silence inspired or inflicted silence upon the students as well, who were aquiver with interest, sensing it was news of some import and hoping it was news of freedom, or at least of a break in routine. And it was such news, there would be no more class that day, or not with me. My father had fallen ill, I read, suddenly and gravely; he was in danger, he might be dying, and he had asked that I come to him, despite the fact that we hadn't spoken in years. When I read this I looked helplessly at the woman next to me, unable to speak. She reached out her hand, saying It's all right, go, I'll stay with them, that's why I came, speaking in Bulgarian as she always did in front of students, she was embarrassed of her English. I managed to thank her, I think, and I murmured something to the class, an apology perhaps, I'm not sure, and then I left the room, the woman, the students eager for news, the sentence that now would never be taken back up; I left the room and descended the broad stairs and stepped out into the scorching day. Though it was September and fall already the sun beat like a bell upon the streets, the grass was dry, the trees seemed withered in their shells; but I walked without thinking, barely noticing the heat. I must have passed the august, slightly crumbling buildings of my school, the Soviet blocks of the police academy, the gate with its guards, the dogs curled in the shade beside it; I must have passed them though I have no memory of them now. I was seeing something else, images that burst in on me, scenes from a childhood I hadn't thought of for years; I had worked hard to forget them but now they came all at once, too quickly to make any sense of them. It was only after I reached Ma-linov, the main boulevard, with its lanes of cars stalled miserably in the heat, that this procession of images began to slow and settle, resolving into more distinct scenes of the life I had left behind. I saw my grandparents' farm, my father lying in a large field used as pasture, I saw myself lying beside him. It was late, and I think it was summer, the night was cool but I could feel the ground releasing the day's heat beneath me, its long exhalation. I remember the freedom I felt, awake far past my bedtime, and my father too was free, having set aside for once the work that filled his days and nights. He was the only one in his family who had gone to college, he studied law and moved to the city, and though it wasn't far from where he and my mother had been born, it was a different world. He hated going back to their small town, to the poverty and dirt he had worked so hard to escape; he only visited once or twice a year, though my mother took us to see her family often, it was important to know where we came from, she said. Her family were small farmers, poor, and though I loved visiting them I knew my life would always be different from theirs, my father made sure I knew it. After the summers we spent on the farm we came back speaking like them, my brother and I, we'd say ain't and y'all and my father would snap at us, angry in a way I didn't understand; Don't talk like that, he'd say, I didn't raise you to talk like that. When we complained about how often he was gone, how much time he spent at his office or away for work, he told us to be grateful, he said we were lucky he worked so hard, we didn't know how lucky, he was giving us a better life than what he'd had. It was rare for him to set aside his work as he did that night, lying with me in the field, when I was still young enough to be a part of him, to touch and be touched by him. It must have been summer, the night was vivid with sounds, with insects and frogs and the low murmurings of cattle; they were familiar sounds and yet every night I was surprised by them, by their density and nearness, like a heavy quilt drawn close. It was dark as it never was in the city, and if I had been alone I would have been frightened, I think, I wasn't a brave child; but my father lay beside me, large and warm in the grass, resting his head back pillowed on his hands. I mimicked this posture as I listened to his voice direct me to the stars and their patterns, which I could never pick out, the patterns and the names that I loved, some of them strange and others homely, Cassiopeia, I recited, the Big Dipper and the Little Bear. I was in my father's confidence, I felt, in the warm thick of it, and so it didn't frighten me to think of the stars and the millions of years it had been since that light was made, even the very light that rained down on us now; nor did it frighten me to think of the dark through which it passed or the dark (my father said) from which it had come, the star itself having gone dark already, perhaps, having ceased to produce the light that reached us and would continue to reach us for millions of years; or maybe then (the voice still spoke but not I thought to me) it would fall where there was no one to receive it, the orphaned light, maybe it would rain on barrenness, our human kind having gone somewhere else, or maybe having disappeared altogether. Surely I only imagine now, from this distance, that there was longing in his voice as he spoke, surely I didn't hear it then, when I turned to him and put my arms around him and buried my face in his chest, as I was still young enough to do, when he wrapped his arms around me in turn, holding me even as I could feel him withdraw into his own reverie or contemplation. But I do hear it, the longing I think he felt as he drifted away from me and from the scene we inhabited together, which must have seemed so different to him, for whom it was the life he had escaped. It was only six months or so before the day when I left my classroom and walked into the September heat that I learned fully both the extent of his longing and the full measure of what he had fled. My sisters had come to visit me in Sofia, my half sisters, the two daughters my father had with his second wife. They were more than a decade younger than I, and I had always felt an overwhelming tenderness for them, which competed with the envy I felt of the love my father showed them so freely. This was especially true of the youngest, G., whom my father loved as he had loved none of the rest of us; he delighted in her swiftness when she was a child, the way she sped about the house, quieting only when he caught her and gathered her in his arms. It was G. who one night told us the stories he had shared with her, stories I couldn't re-member ever having heard, though occasionally some note in what she said struck as if at a distance a familiar tone. We hadn't seen one another for years, and in that time my father's second marriage had failed, ending what had always seemed to me my sisters' good fortune. One of them was just out of college, the other still studying, and I was shocked at the sight of them; they were competent and adult, elegant, with a sophistication I could never dream of having. We were in the main room of my apartment, the common room and kitchen, surrounded by the detritus of a gathering we had had; we sat with half a bottle of wine, two of us at the table and G. alone on the couch. We had let the room go almost dark, only a few candles were still burning, and through the windows the lights of the neighboring *blokove* were lovely, now that the gray of their concrete had faded into the night. It was my birthday, we had all been drinking, but G. with an abandon I watched with concern. She had arrived a few days before my other sister, and each night we spent alone together she stayed up drinking long after I had gone exhausted to bed. There was a note of defiance in how she drank, an assertion of adulthood, but also something desperate, I thought, an escape either from or to. Her estrangement from my father was recent enough that the loss still held a kind of electric charge for her, so that at times as we spoke I thought I could see her jerk with the pang of it. All my life, she told me in those first nights we spent together, speaking with the wonder of someone for whom the examination of life still offers the promise of revelation or escape; all my life I've lived to please him, she said, every choice I've made has been his choice, it's like nothing I've ever wanted has been my own. So what do I do now, she asked, how do I even know what I want to do? She had always been driven; as a child she worked harder than any of the rest of us in school, she excelled at sports, she was the president of her class, in everything she did she was exceptional. She questioned all of it now, she said, everything she had done, everything she had wanted, not just these public ambitions but also more private needs. We had never talked about sex before; she was so much younger and I had always shied away from it, though she knew something about my own history from the poems I had published, which she searched out and read with an attention they seldom, probably in no other case received. I just wanted to get it over with, she said about the first time she had sex, it was a relief, I didn't want it to be a big deal. She was fourteen when she started sneaking out at night, she told me, boys would wait for her, their cars running on the next street over; they were always older guys, she said, first seniors at her school and then college students she met at parties. I'd lie about my age, she said, I'd say I was sixteen or seventeen and they'd believe me, or maybe they just pretended to believe me. It's not like there were that many of them, she said, seeing the dismay I felt, I didn't even have sex with all of them, I just liked being with them, I liked the attention. I don't know why I cringed at her stories, when I had done so much worse at her age, having sex in parks and bathrooms, dangerous and indiscriminate sex; but I was troubled that her history seemed to parallel my own, that we shared what I had thought of as my own gnawing affliction. And I knew she would outgrow the satisfactions she had found, that soon she would desire other and more intense experiences, drawn forward by those appetites we share, that humiliating need that has always, even in my moments of apparent pride, run alongside my life like a snapping dog. Even these desires, I thought as I listened to my sister, seemed to descend from my father like an inherited disease. It was my father we spoke of that night after our party, as we always did when we were together; but now my sisters' anger had changed, their mother had told them about my father's cruelty, about his many affairs and her sense of abandonment. But G. already knew about those affairs, she said, she had known about them for a long time. She was very young, she told us, when she discovered my father's infidelities, which already were unsettling her life, accounting for so much of the tension and noise around her, her parents' incessant quarrels. She was thirteen or fourteen when she came upon the cache of Internet sites and chat rooms he visited; he hadn't even bothered to hide them, my sister said, there wasn't any password to crack, she had found them really without looking, less curious than bored as she clicked through files. It was his computer, but she was allowed to use it from time to time, so it wasn't exactly forbidden territory she wandered when almost by accident she stumbled upon images he had saved, hundreds of them, she said, showing men with women, or two women alone. It was as though he had filed them by some logic of progression, the images growing ever more obscene and upsetting, little pageants of submission and need. It never occurred to her to go to her mother with what she had found, she said; she had already been enlisted in her parents' battles, subjected to the cruelty of sparring adults in relation to their children, a cruelty that reduces those children to tools or weapons, to weapons of a particularly brutal kind. He had made her his partisan, her first thought was to protect him, and so she wasn't only aware of what he was doing but implicated in it, that was the word she used, implicated. But it wasn't only that, I imagined, it wasn't just keeping his secrets that implicated her; I thought there must have been another fascination too as she told us how she went back again and again to his store of images, tracking how it changed, its additions and substitutions. And soon she wanted more, she became devious, she installed a program on his computer that recorded everything he typed. What, she said, seeing my surprise, it's easy, there are a million of them, you just download one from the Internet, and I had to laugh, despite her story and the disquiet I felt. She could follow his tracks now, she went on, she had the passwords for the pages that had been locked, chat rooms and hookup sites, and not only that; in these new records she could pull up transcripts of his conversations, or not conversations exactly, since she could only see his side of them, a solitary voice calling out its desires. She read his profiles, the various selves he fashioned, all of them a mixture of the real and the ideal. Sometimes he said he was single, sometimes he lied about his age, in one he used a picture that was a decade old. It was ridiculous, she said, who did he think he was kidding, you could tell it was an old picture. There was one site that was for married men, there was a market for them, she said, can you imagine? It was on this page that he came closest to telling the truth about his life, and among his enticements he listed his children, our accomplishments, the good schools and awards, the ways we had all sought to please him; all of it was laid out like grotesquely splayed plumage. But what she went back for, she said abruptly, as if catching hold again of her thought, were the transcripts her program produced, their record of each key struck. She read these lines with fascination and disgust, she said, watching my father's fantasies played out before her in skeletal form, the pleading tones, the boasts and commands clear even through the poorly typed lines, the symbols and abbreviations of Internet chat that make such language seem so much like a process of decay. As I listened to her, I imagined (imagining myself in her place) that she couldn't help but provide the missing voice, inventing the invitations and evasions that his own lines responded to or provoked, until it must have felt as if she had become part of those dramas, I imagined, how could she not. She followed his conversations for months, she told us, checking them every few days. I should have known it was going to happen, she said, I mean I did know, I guess I was waiting for it, but she was still surprised when it became clear that he had taken one of these conversations offline. He was actually fucking one of them, my sister said, grimacing at the words, he wasn't just dicking around online. And now, since she still hadn't said a word about what she knew, she didn't just feel complicit, she told us, but guilty of a crime. She became more difficult with her mother, they fought all the time, she said, she felt pity and disgust for her, she wasn't sure which she felt more. He never just chatted with one woman, she went on, he was always chatting with several of them at once. He was polite sometimes, sweet, but he could be rude, too, he was rough with some of them, it was like he was a different person with each one. It was like that for me, too, I thought as I listened

to her, it's one of the things I crave in the sites I use, that I can
carry on these multiple conversations, each its own window
so that sometimes my screen is filled with them; and in each
I have the sense of being entirely false and entirely true, like
a self in a story, I suppose, or the self I inhabit when I teach,
the self of authority and example. I know they're all I have,
these partial selves, true and false at once, that any ideal of
wholeness I long for is a sham; but I do long for it, I think I
glimpse it sometimes, I even imagine I've felt it. Maybe it's
an illusion but I think I did feel this wholeness in the field
with my father, alone and with the night surrounding us,
and my father was necessary to it even as he withdrew into
his own longings, as I imagine now, contemplating the stars
that I contemplated beside him, though I was contemplating
him perhaps more than the stars. His withdrawal didn't
diminish our closeness but deepened it, it was a sign of
vulnerability and trust, like an animal turning its back. I
emerged from these thoughts to find myself on a small street
deep among the *blokove*, which rose stark on both sides twelve
or thirteen stories, the length of city blocks, their blankness
relieved by graffiti and, higher up, by lines of laundry hung
out in the sun, as well as by fissures and patches where the
facades had cracked. As I walked a narrow path between
the buildings and the cars that were parked nose-first almost against their walls, like nursing cats, I looked into the
dim boxes framed by the windows I passed, apartments
identical in size and shape though none of them was exactly
the same. I was walking quickly and only glimpsed them,
but in each there was some distinguishing feature, a flower
box or patterned curtains or small panes of colored glass hung
to catch the light, attempts at beauty, I thought, or at least
signs of care. Almost all of the rooms were empty, but in a
few there were solitary figures, old men or women, sometimes absorbed in some task but mostly just sitting and fan-

ning themselves, staring at little televisions or simply staring, their faces turned to the windows I passed, so that our eyes met for a moment and I saw their vacancy liven and shift, like still water ruffled by a stone. It was a balm of which I was unaware, the safety I felt as I lay with my father, and it sustained me throughout his many absences, even, a few years later, when he left my mother and was unreachable for months, and then reappeared in a new home where we were welcome only on invitation. Even after my parents separated, though they occurred less and less frequently, I still had these moments of closeness with my father. Until I was eight or nine I enjoyed an access to his physical presence free of suspicion or doubt, even as I grew aware of the differences between his body and mine, aware of them and interested, troubled perhaps and drawn to that trouble, so that what had been our games (the race to the toilet after a long drive, pissing in the tight space pressed together) became occasions of greater and greater solemnity and unease, possessed of a mystery I couldn't resolve. This was happening with my friends, too, the boys whose company I sought out with a new urgency, and though it was still slight and free of intention they could sense the added heat. They were starting to think of me as a kind apart, and what was a shadow of separation between us would become absolute, I felt it already with a terrible dread. I don't remember how old I was when I realized the full measure of that separateness, I must have been nine or ten, still young enough to shower with my father, though it happened less often now and excited me more, in the mysterious way that would lead to the still unimagined breach I was already approaching. Though I can't remember the season or year or anything that was said, I remember the room, the ornamental bulbs and the tile and the water already running, the mirror obscured with fog; and I remember my father, his body large and bare, the fascination of it and its availability in the small space where, laughing, we wrestled to stay beneath the hot stream of water. I was old enough to wash myself but we still touched each other; he would ask me to wash his back, which was difficult for him to reach, and then he would wash mine in turn. Though he was often severe and sometimes cruel he was gentle with me there; if the soap ran into my eyes he would rinse them, tilting my face up with his hand, a kind of physical care he seldom undertook. We had stepped out of the water onto the tiles, which could be slick, he reminded me each time, Be careful, he said, and then I approached him, not with any specific intent but perhaps not innocently either, I can't be sure after so many years, as I can no longer recall whether he was facing me or looking away, though he must have been looking away or he would have stopped me or avoided my touch. Or maybe it's more true to say I was innocent but not without intent, what was it but an intention that drove me, a bodily intention; I wanted to touch him, not with an outcome in mind but with an ache, perhaps not an intention but an ache, which drove me to him and which he felt, too, when I put my arms around him and pressed my body to his and he felt my erection where it touched him. That was the end of care, he thrust me away without a thought for the slickness of the tiles; and when I looked at his face, which was twisted in disgust, it was as if I saw his true face, his authentic face, not the learned face of fatherhood. He covered himself quickly and left the room, saying nothing, but his look entered me and settled there and has never left, it rooted beneath memory and became my understanding of myself, my understanding and expectation. From that day, all the ease we had enjoyed together was gone. He took away the safety I had felt, the certainty of my bond with my father, the first bond; until that day I hadn't realized it could be dissolved like any other. And it was as though I lost something of myself as well, as though I became somehow less real as my father withdrew from me, less substantial or less certain of my substance, as though I too were something that might dissolve. It still shows me to myself, that look, I saw it again as I walked among the *blokove* without thinking of where I walked. The sun was high and already I was dripping with sweat, the page I had been given was a damp ball in my hand. It would be years before my father spoke the words that finally severed the bond between us, but there were no more showers or games. Nor could I find anywhere else the closeness I had taken for granted: the friends I turned to were scared off by the need I felt for them, and soon the best I could hope for was their indifference. It was then that I retreated into the uneasy solitude from which I've never entirely emerged. Only once did I let myself imagine I had found again the closeness I had lost, and this memory too returned as I walked through a part of Mladost I had never seen. The *blokove* had grown sparse, there were larger plots of wasteland between them and also abandoned hulks of construction, huge concrete frames rising up like excavated ruins or ships rotting at sea. Every surface was covered with graffiti, mindless obscenities or slogans or art of a strangely childlike incompetence, affecting in its incompetence; and though the area must have been inhabited, this graffiti was the only evidence I had seen for some time of living human presence, the graffiti and also, where branches overhung the concrete, adhesive puddles like tar where fruit had ripened and fallen and been trodden to pulp, drawing large black birds that clawed and pried at it and rose up clamoring at my approach. It was like a land of ravens, if that's what they were, of ravens and of dogs, which are everywhere in Sofia but were rougher and more numerous here; they were battered, vicious things, more desperate than the dogs where I lived. A few made as if to lunge when I startled them, bracing themselves and snarling in a way that would usually have alarmed me but that now I took in stride, ready to meet them, ready myself to lunge should it come to that; I was eager for it, even, and maybe this eagerness was what kept them in check. There were dogs of all types and a range of sizes, though it was clear a certain bulk was necessary for survival, and most were muscular and medium-sized, with bullish features and square jaws, solid dogs with a brutal elegance that appealed to me, as did their short coats, mottled and tawny, so that as they slept they looked like fawns curled in the unmown grasses. Not all of the dogs were hostile, some were friendly enough, emerging to trot beside me for a few steps, swinging their low tails. Normally I would have felt sympathy for them, especially for the gentlest of them, a beautiful dog that trotted beside me longer than the others and that bore an extraordinary scar along his right side. The skin had been ripped open and had unevenly healed; it was puckered and hairless and raw, as if something had half melted the flesh along the whole length of him. It was a terrible scar, from an injury he was lucky to have survived, and yet he was the least savage of the dogs, the most eager for my attention; at one point he even nudged against my hand with his nose, the hand in which I held the news of my father. It was cruel not to acknowledge him but I didn't acknowledge him, and I had the sense that he stuck with me as long as he dared before he reached some invisible border and turned back. I didn't turn back, I walked farther, to the very edge of habitation, where the *blokove* gave out finally at the rim of a steep hill. Down the embankment there were grasses and scattered trees and beyond the trees a huge clearing extending for kilometers; and on the other side of the clearing there was another district of concrete towers, so that it was like a bay, the half ring of *blokove* braced against the grasses like waters. Where I stood the pavement was broken, marking an uncertain border, a not quite wild place; and then suddenly without deciding to I was making my way down the steep bank. It was difficult to climb down, especially in the shoes I had been wearing in the classroom, black dress shoes of the sort my father had taught me to take care of when I was a child, polishing them until they shone. They were a sign of who I was, he said, and I was never careful enough, I would forget I was wearing them and run with them on, they would get dirty or scuffed and he would say I had no sense of the worth of things, or worse that I had no pride, the pride it was incumbent upon me as his son to have. It was difficult to stay upright as the ground beneath me shifted, and soon my shoes were caked with mud from gouging the side of the hill. For years after that day in the shower, there was nothing to replace the closeness I had lost with my father, and more and more I took refuge in books, not serious or significant books but books that offered an escape from myself, and it was these books, or rather our shared love for them, that bound me to the few friends I had and that laid the ground for my friendship with K. He was from my city but our paths had never crossed, he lived in another part of town and went to a different school. But we had friends in common, and one of them suggested we should know each other. He called me one afternoon when K. was visiting his house; You like the same writers, he said, and then he handed K. the phone. It would be months before we met in person, and in those months our conversations grew longer and more frequent, until they became, I think for both of us, the primary fact of our lives; sometimes we talked the whole night long, as one does only in adolescence or very early in love. I was happy, but also I felt an anxiety that gnawed at me and for which I could find no cause, that gnawed at me more deeply precisely because I could find no cause. For months our friendship consisted of nothing but words, and though I wanted to see him this was a comfort; already I felt that the best of me was words, that it was in words our friendship would flourish. Soon we had told each other everything about ourselves, all our stories, multiple times, and I never tired of them, of them or of his voice as he spoke them. I wanted to see him but it frightened me, too, the thought of meeting him, of K. seeing the body that increasingly felt alien to me, outsized and malformed, that in no way conformed to my sense of myself, to the self I lived inwardly. But we did finally meet in person, in October, at the very end of the month. It was a kind of Indian summer, the mildness of it a surprise and a pleasure. I was living in the basement of my father's house, having been tossed between houses many times, a consequence of my parents' wrangling, which hadn't ended, they were in and out of court for years. When K.'s mother dropped him off we were shy at first, it took a moment for me to reconcile the voice I knew with the boy before me, who was shorter than I and thin, with red hair he let hang over his eyes and a face that was beautiful and pale and streaked with acne. We had chosen my house over K.'s because we would have more privacy and freedom there, and if we had no real plans for the use of these things we had an instinctive preference for them. My father gave us a wide berth, having always been ill at ease around children, around anyone at all unknown, and after he shook K.'s hand he left us to ourselves. He had ordered pizza for us, and we ate it in my basement room, talking and laughing with each other. We had all the freedom we could want and yet we waited for even greater freedom, for my father and stepmother to retreat to the upper floor of the house and leave the large middle floor between us empty. And then, when we thought they were sleeping, we slipped into the garage, where it was easy to pop the large mechanical door free of its mechanism and then slide it up slowly, silently or nearly silently, just enough for us to crawl on our stomachs through. I did this almost every night, though there was no reason for it, I had nowhere to go, we lived in the suburbs and every street was the same. Nor was there any point to the secrecy, since by that time my father had largely if not yet finally washed his hands of me and I could do as I liked. But it was crucial somehow that I sneak out, that I disappear from my room without anyone knowing, beyond the reach of the authority I chafed under at every other moment of the day, at school and at home; it was only out on these walks that I felt I could relax the guard I kept at every other moment. Whatever the weather I went out and wandered, and now I wandered with K.; I introduced him to my solitude and he deepened it without disturbance. We clambered down the steep hill from my father's house, which towered over the whole neighborhood, a sign of how far he had come. It was the night before Halloween and so there was, this once, something to look at in the streets, the houses had been decorated for the holiday, each more elaborately than the last. Trees had become the habitations of ghosts, there were scarecrows and jack-o'-lanterns and ghouls of every kind, whole covens of plastic witches danced in ragged clothes. It was tawdry and crass and all of it an invitation to mischief. We imagined stealing decorations from one yard and placing them in another, we thought up obscene arrangements—but we left all of it undone, the joy was in the planning of it, in our own inventiveness, and we bent over choking on our hushed laughter, having brought each other to tears. But there were other decorations, too, more strident ones: it was an election year and there were campaign signs among the ghosts and cauldrons, an odd juxtaposition of playfulness and belligerence. For months

the news had been full of debate and raised voices, and my
house was full of them, too; my father loved to hold forth
and for the first time I had begun to challenge him, wanting an opinion of my own. It was as though every word
I said was a provocation, every discussion became a quarrel;
though he gave me a wide berth we still collided and our
collisions were a kind of theater, like animals locking horns.
It was a Republican state and my father held the expected
views, like everyone else he knew, or so it seemed to me;
but K. and I agreed, we hated my father's party, and we
were both angered by the signs in the yards, nearly all of
them echoing the same names. K. approached one of these
signs and kicked it, bending its wire legs a bit, and then he
pulled it from the ground and ripped it and threw the torn
halves back on the grass. I was shocked at first, but then I
was delighted, and I grabbed a sign of my own. We took
turns for a while and then enthusiasm or impatience took
over; K. chose one side of the street and I the other, and
we went methodically house by house, wrecking all of the
signs in sight, pretending perhaps it was something else we
wrecked. As we walked away, laughing again, K. hung his
arm around my neck. It was a casual gesture but one I wasn't
used to, and I was almost frightened by the happiness that
overtook me, that filled me up and charged me and at the
same time carried a threat; it was too unrestrained, there
was nothing to keep it in check. I felt solid again as I
walked with him, more certain of myself than I had been
for years, with his arm around my neck and my own slung
at his waist. We knocked against each other but what did
it matter, there was no one to see us, we moved with an
awkward freedom but a freedom nonetheless. My father's
house was close to the neighborhood where I was born and
where my mother still lived; he moved there with his new
wife a few months after he left my mother, who became as

much a part of his past as the poverty and dirt of my grand-parents' farm. Though our walk had seemed aimless, in fact I was leading us to my mother's street and the house I had grown up in, which I wanted K. to see, as though in the very architecture there were some further revelation I could make. We didn't need to go in, it was enough to stand on the sidewalk looking at the large house in which my mother now lived alone; I pointed out my window to him, or what had been my window, which was dark like all the others. And then I led him farther along the long street circling the neighborhood (though I haven't walked it for years I can walk it now, I can see the very cracks in the stone) as it curved and led us to my first school, a squat ugly building of concrete slabs and bricks. It was a part of my history and I wanted it to be his as well, the grounds, the diminutive athletic fields, the tree-bordered fence with its dried vines of honeysuckle. We were in no hurry, no one knew where we were and there was no reason to rush back, so we sat for a while on the swings in the playground. We didn't really swing in them, we just sat and talked, rocking a little side by side; I had talked for a long time and mostly K. talked now, and since we had nothing new to say to each other he repeated the stories that I loved for him to tell. I leaned back, holding on to the chains as I looked up at the subur-ban sky that was like dull metal or unvarnished wood, the few stars making none of the patterns I had been taught were there. And then I leaned back too far, I lost my balance and the plastic seat slipped out from under me, and I fell onto the dirt beneath. K. stopped talking, biting off his sentence, and then we both started to laugh, and K. leaned back and let himself fall, too, hitting the ground beside me. We kept laughing, with our backs in the dirt and our legs still hooked through the swings, and I felt the same happi-ness mixed with fear, as though I were being offered a nourishment that might, now I had tasted it, be denied. Finally we stopped laughing, we rose and brushed the dirt from our clothes. We had been walking for hours when we got back to my father's house, and as we slid beneath the door again we complained that our feet and our legs hurt, and K. said his back hurt as well. We were both exhausted and we fell gratefully onto the bed in the main room; it was a waterbed and we laughed again as we fell onto it, it knocked us up and down and we grabbed on both to the frame and to each other to steady ourselves. We managed to find our balance and keep the mattress still, or not quite still exactly, even turning our heads made it wobble, but though we were tired neither of us was in the mood to sleep. We lay beside each other, as always endlessly talking, and then K. complained about his back again, asking if I would rub it for him. He rolled over to give me access but it was impossible on the bed, when I applied my weight the mattress just gave way beneath him, he said he didn't feel anything, and so he got up and sat down on the wooden frame, placing his feet on the ground and turning his back to me. But he still wasn't comfortable, he asked me to reach beneath his shirt and rub the skin itself, and I did, I gripped his shoulders and kneaded them, I applied pressure until he hissed and then I eased off. I worked his neck and down the column of his spine, the muscles bunched on either side, and maybe for the first time in our friendship our constant chatter had ceased. I had never touched anyone in that way before, I wanted to keep touching him, and I was dismayed when K. shifted his weight, I thought he had had enough and was getting up. But instead he began to lean back, so slowly that I was confused at first and resisted him, pressing my hands more firmly against his back; it was only when he insisted that I understood and allowed him to lean into me, as he pressed farther leaning back in turn, so that we fell

slowly backward until we were lying on the bed again, I on
the bed and K. on me. I hadn't taken my hands out from
under his shirt, I had reached around him as he lay back,
and now I held him in an embrace that if he didn't return
he didn't reject, either, he received it, he let his head fall
back against my chest and we lay like that for a while. Then
he shifted again, or maybe I did, and we were lying beside
each other. He was holding me now or we were holding each other; I was turned toward him, pressed against his
back with my arms still around him, and where my hands met
at his chest he crossed his own arms over them. For a long time
we lay without moving, and as we half slept I was conscious
of touching him, of his stomach where my fingers curled
beneath his shirt. In the center of his abdomen there was
a line where the sheets of muscle met, a rivulet or ridge that
I traced with the pads of my fingers; it was covered very
lightly with hair, impossibly soft and fine, like the skin of
certain fruit. It was a boy's body, I realize now, we were
younger it occurs to me even than my students; but K.'s
body didn't seem to me in any way incomplete or less than
fully formed, I couldn't imagine anything more perfect,
he was entirely beautiful. It didn't occur to me to want
more from that moment, to test it and see how far it might
be stretched; it didn't occur to me to touch him in some
way other than I touched him, or at least I don't remember it now. We did sleep more soundly eventually, we must
have, since I woke early the next morning to find that K.
was ill. He was on his hands and knees beside the bed, as
though he had fallen there, and it was the sound of his
moans that had woken me. I could see that he had vomited
and now he vomited again; it must have been something we
ate, I thought, though we had eaten together and I wasn't
ill at all. He groaned again, with a sound that was almost a
sob, and then seeing I was awake he apologized, I wasn't

sure for what, whether for waking me or for the mess he had made. His forehead was beaded with sweat, and when I placed my hand on his back the thin fabric of his shirt was damp. I kept my hand there as his back heaved with the gulping nauseous breaths he drew, until he shrugged me off and pushed me away as he vomited again, each of his convulsions accompanied by a moan or a sob. I was helpless, I wanted to take care of him but I didn't know how, and when he was calm again I asked him what he wanted. I want to go home, he said, still on his hands and knees, and so I left him there to go find my father. I knew he was already awake, I had heard him moving on the floor above us, and when I opened the door at the top of the stairs I found him in the kitchen alone. He was standing at the sink with his back to the door, and though he must have heard me coming up the stairs he didn't turn to greet or acknowledge me, not even when I began to speak. It was barely dawn, he was watching the first light rise through the window above the sink, a moment of quiet I interrupted when I told him that K. was sick, that he needed to go home. Could he drive us, I asked, and then I added as I always did with my father a kind of apology, so that even before he answered I had apologized for asking. All right, he said, and though he didn't move from the window or turn around I understood that I should hurry to get us ready, that having disturbed my father I shouldn't also make him wait. I went back downstairs to K., who was calmer now; he had risen from his knees to the edge of the bed, where he was bracing himself with his hands. He thought he would be all right on the ride, he said, he just wanted to be home, he would feel better there. I took towels from the bathroom and began to clean up his mess, which shamed me somehow, I didn't want my father to see it. When K. moved as if to help me I motioned him back, though I could see that he was ashamed too, that he was mortified to have me clean up after him. Please, he said, but I motioned him back, I couldn't say exactly why, I told him to get his things together instead. My father had gone up to his bedroom to get dressed and now he was coming back down, we could hear his bulk on the upper stairs. K. was thrusting his few things into his bag when the door opened and my father appeared at the top of the hall, rattling his keys. Hurriedly I dropped a towel over the vomit I had yet to mop up, thinking that if I could do nothing about the smell I could at least hide the sight of it away. As he opened the door to the garage (the same door we had left through a few hours before), my father said I'm sorry you're not well, or something like it, something neighborly, the sort of thing one says, and K. thanked him as we got into the car, my father alone in front and K. and I together in the back. As if by instinct we sat well apart, and though I couldn't help glancing at him we said nothing to each other. Shortly into the ride I realized I could still smell him, not only his vomit but his body, too, his sweat, which was bitter and strong; I was embarrassed for my father to smell it. I lowered the window a little and laid my head against the glass. The air was cool as it flooded in but the foulness still remained, and though K. had always before filled me with joy he seemed part of my shame now and of the foulness in the air, not just a bodily foulness but something stranger and heavier. My father glanced at us often in the mirror, a quick flick of the eyes. K. sat with his face to the window but I thought he must feel it too, that watchfulness and the weight it added to the air. It was the watchfulness that made it foul, I realized, not with its own foulness but with a foulness it found in us. K. turned away from the window but didn't look at me, and when I asked him if he was all right he didn't answer, though when my father asked him the same question, the very same, as though he hadn't heard me ask it or as though it were a different question from his lips, K. spoke, he said Yes, sir, and I felt him turn from me, in that foul air I felt him identify me as foulness. It was as though he felt my father was health and I contagion, and I was at once bewildered by this and unsurprised. Those were the only words they shared; for the rest of the drive we were silent, and it wasn't until we arrived at K.'s house that he glanced my way and nodded, and then he thanked my father and got out of the car and hurried inside the door his mother held open. My father waved at her, leaning across to the passenger-side window, and then he reversed the car and slid out of the driveway as I turned to look at the door that closed behind K. When the car stopped for a light at the end of the street, I looked again at the mirror where I could see my father's face. He was watching me, not with the flickering surveillance of moments before but steadily, and when my eyes met his he grimaced, as if he could still smell K., though there wasn't any smell in the air anymore. I stared back at him. For a moment I thought he was going to speak and I steeled myself, I saw his face harden with what he would say; but instead he saw that the light had changed and began driving again, and I let my head fall back against the window, watching the streets as they passed. I had been ready to accuse my father of what he had done, the disgust he had shared with K., and I felt my anger again as I walked through the grass in that undeveloped space I hadn't known was there. The wastes of Mladost, I had often said about the whole blighted district, but this was a genuine wasteland; people threw their trash down the hill, not just bottles and cans but tires and bricks and, in one spot, a mound of broken concrete that a truck must have poured out from above. Everywhere else I had walked had been dry, the ground beside the pavement parched and hard, but here my shoes sank into the soil. I was thick in the grasses that from a distance had looked like waters, the grasses like a bay and the *blokove* like land, and still I walked without any destination in mind. K. and I remained friends for a while after that day, but we never had another night like that first; we were more reserved with each other, we didn't speak for hours on end anymore, or with the same freedom. Over the next weeks he called me less often, and when I called him he was almost never home. He had met a girl, he said, and when we did speak he spoke about her, he told me every word they said to each other, every gesture they made. As he cataloged his feelings I tried to meet him as I always had in his words, but I couldn't now, they were like a territory he receded into and that excluded me. He told me about every victory and frustration, the teasing games she played, how she made him wait for everything he wanted, and how even her delays delighted him, so long as he was sure that they would end. But increasingly as the weeks passed K. was frustrated by a delay beyond their control, by his mother's vigilance, her denial of the privacy they craved. She was always watching them, K. said, she insisted his door remain open, they could be interrupted at any time; and they couldn't go to her house, either, her father was even more strict, there they couldn't even kiss; and it was winter now, even if they could find a suitable place outside, secluded, romantic, it was impossible, it was bitterly cold. If they had cars it would be different, he said, when you have a car you always have privacy, but we didn't have cars, we were still too young to drive. It was after this inventory of impossibilities that he told me he thought I could help him, if I didn't mind, as of course I didn't; I was grateful he would ask me for help, it would bring us closer again, I thought. I would do anything for him, I said, and what he asked was nothing, just that I come to his house and be present, simply be there with him and his girlfriend in his room. His mother wouldn't be so vigilant then, they would have some uninterrupted time, and if they weren't quite alone it would be the next best thing. I was his best friend, he said. And she wouldn't mind either, the girl he said now that he loved; he had told her everything about me and she wanted to meet me, he said, she understood why I had to be there, she wanted it as much as he did. Please, he said again, though I had already agreed, the repetition a kind of courtesy; of course I would help him, I said, in this as in everything. And so the following weekend I met K.'s girlfriend, about whom I had heard so much I felt I already knew her, though we were still awkward and reserved with each other when we met in the kitchen of K.'s house. His mother handed us our drinks and made a general fuss of welcome, while of course all we wanted was to be left alone, to claim our privacy, which I anticipated with eager dread and for which K. I knew was simply eager. He fidgeted in his seat, glancing first at me and then at her, holding my gaze though he didn't hold hers, as though he couldn't bear to look at her for long. I was safer, he could share with me what he felt, and if this wasn't the intimacy we had known or that I craved it was still a kind of intimacy, which I could be part of even if it wasn't exactly mine. He drummed his fingers on the table, he shuffled his feet beneath it. We had already introduced ourselves, K.'s girlfriend and I; she was slight and blond and unremarkably pretty, smiling at me with her big teeth. I had resisted liking her but I did like her, she was kind and wanted my friendship, she had heard so much, she said, she had been waiting so long to meet me. Her name was K., which was something they joked about, their sharing of the initial: K. and K., they said, laughing, making a kind of music of their names, K. and K. They already had jokes of their own, which made them laugh even in front of K.'s mother, who laughed

at them too. Even in her presence it was clear what they felt
for each other, their feelings were bright and open, sure of
their place; if there were certain obstacles to be overcome
they were just for show, scenery for a drama everyone would
applaud. Even their parents would applaud it, they only pretended to disapprove, when what they really felt was indulgence and pride and the sweetness of youth, their own youth
that they could remember and relive and sanction. K.'s
mother finally allowed us upstairs, though she admonished
us as well, telling me to keep an eye on things, to make them
behave; she was trusting me, she said, pointing her finger at
me jokingly, though she wasn't joking, I thought, and I said
Yes, ma'am, as though I too were part of the rightness of
the world. We walked up the narrow corridor of the stairs
in single file, K.'s girlfriend first and then K. and then I, and
once we were out of sight their hands reached out for each
other. As I walked behind them I felt an excitement that was
deep and unsettling and, alongside this, a dread that increased
as we neared K.'s room. I paused, as if to weigh what I felt,
but when K.'s voice called out for me I hurried up the final
stairs, turning the corner to see him at the door looking for
me quizzically. Come on, he said, still eager, more eager now,
and then his face broke into a grin and I forgot my dread. I
moved past him into the small room where K. already sat
on the bed, crossing and recrossing her legs. I moved toward
the only other seat, the wooden chair at K.'s desk, but he
stopped me, asking me to wait a minute as he closed the
door, or didn't close it, exactly, which his mother had forbidden, but left it as little ajar as he dared. Then he asked me
to sit in front of it, if I didn't mind; since the door opened
into the room I could make sure they wouldn't be surprised,
I might hear his mother coming and I could take my time
getting up, delaying her while they composed themselves.
Again he apologized, he knew it was an imposition, I would

have to sit on the floor; but of course I didn't object, I welcomed it, it was a service I could provide. And also it meant that I could watch them, since with my back to the door I would face his bed. I had never been in his room before, which was unremarkable, any teenager's room, with books and his boxy computer and posters of soccer stars on the walls. The only object in it of any interest at all was the bed on which they sat, the two K.s, which was unmade, the sheets tangled at its foot where he had kicked them off, and I remembered with sudden sharpness the heat of his body beside me as we slept. We talked for a while, K. wanted to get to know me, she said, and she drew me out, but as she and I talked K. was silent. He was frustrated, I realized, he didn't want us to talk; but K. insisted, when I fell silent she drew me out again, asking about my family and my school, about stories she had heard, things she had learned from K. I was stung that he had told her so much, that he had used my stories as a way to strengthen his bond with her: they were secrets we had shared, and now they were secrets he shared with her. She kept talking, making K. wait, which was the point of her questions; it was a way to hold him off, one of the games they played. Finally K. got up from the bed, he went to the stereo on a shelf above the desk and turned on some music, not loud, not with the intention of covering noise but to cover the absence of noise, the absence of talk, which he put a stop to when he sat back down on his bed and placed his hand on K.'s thigh, leaning in and pressing his mouth to hers. She didn't resist him, anything but; she relaxed and allowed him to lean her back against the wall. As they kissed each other I felt something twist in me, something that made me look quickly away to the posters pinned inert to the walls, but I couldn't look away for long, again and again I was drawn back to the sight of them on the bed. I didn't want them to catch me looking but there was no need to worry, their eyes were closed, they were entirely engrossed in each other. I was surprised to see that though K. had toyed and delayed she was leading the action now; it was her hand that dropped into his lap and as I saw it my excitement deepened, my excitement and my dread both. They were still kissing each other, their lips hadn't parted though now K.'s hand was at his belt; all her nervousness was gone, replaced with expertise, or what looked like expertise as she worked to undo it with a single hand. She knew how to please him, I thought as her hand slipped into his jeans, where I could see it moving as she touched him, and could see his erection as well, the shape of it against the cloth. I couldn't stand it suddenly, being in that room with their bodies and the passion joining them at the mouths, I wanted to be anywhere else, though I still couldn't look away. I don't think I had let myself realize until then what I wanted or how much I wanted it. Finally they stopped kissing, K. pulled her mouth away and whispered something in his ear and then lowered her head to his crotch, using both her hands to unbutton his jeans before she placed her mouth where her hand had been. I pulled my knees up and hugged them against my chest. I couldn't see anything, she had turned her head so that her hair hung down like a veil, but I watched frozen as K. put one of his hands on her head and then dropped it to her shoulder, gripping her there. I looked at K.'s face then and saw that he was watching me, that he had seen me watching them and was waiting for me to look up. He caught me and held my gaze without welcome or warmth or any hint of what we had shared, and my sense of having violated something, of having looked where I shouldn't have faded, as I understood that this was what he wanted me to see all along, that I was there not as guard but as audience. I was there to see how different from me he was, how free of the foulness my father had shown him; and now that I had seen it, I knew our friendship had run its course. He closed his eyes then, he gave himself over and with a quick breath sucked between his teeth let his head fall back against the wall. He knew I was watching and he let me watch. It was like a parting gift, I thought as I kept watching his face and the movements it made, it looked almost as if he were in pain. I was in pain too, and almost without thinking I let my hand drop between my legs and gripped myself hard. I've sought it ever since, I think, the combination of exclusion and desire I felt in his room, beneath the pain of exclusion the satisfaction of desire; sometimes I think it's the only thing I've sought. I had been walking away from the base of the hill, into that declivity or bay where all the runoff from the surrounding districts must have run, so that despite the dryness everywhere else the ground here was a morass, I was mired in roots and mud. I couldn't get across, I realized, I was ankle-deep in it already, I had ruined my shoes. I turned back to the base of the hill I had climbed down and continued to walk there, skirting the mud as best I could. It was still hot though the height of the day had passed, the sun beat down but less insistently now. There was no pavement where I walked, no concrete or steel, and it was quiet, there was no human noise at all. I had been thinking for a long time of K. and it wasn't anger I felt for him; if he had been cruel I could understand it, he had been a child, he had reached for what he needed. There was a copse of trees ahead and I aimed for it, quickening my pace, wanting to be out of the sun; I felt the tightness and warmth of my skin now where it had burned, and even the weaker late-afternoon light was painful. As I drew nearer I became aware of a sound, of movement first and then of water, of water flowing swiftly, and soon I could see it too, a light among the trees, a broad low stream sliding shallow over rock. I was surprised to find it here, so close to the *blokove*, I hadn't seen any sign of it as I wandered, and it was as though something in me softened as I walked beside it. I felt grief more than anger now, though I wasn't sure for what exactly, whether for myself or for K., or for the men I had known since him, none of whom I'd loved as fully, few of whom I'd loved at all; and finding it was for all of these things I turned my thoughts to the page that was coming apart as I gripped and regripped it. I thought of my father, old and sick, I imagined him bedridden and frail; I wanted to see if I felt grief for him, too, if my grief extended so far. Were they with him now, I wondered, had my sisters received a similar message, had they softened and gone to him, had G. softened and gone to him? I remembered how angry she had been that night in Mladost, when she told us the stories about my father that were also stories about herself, also stories about me. We had listened to her for a long time, my other sister and I; the last candles had finally gone out, though we could still see ourselves in the light from the street. G. was my father's youngest child, his last child, who (perhaps he thought) finally loved him as he deserved to be loved, and he had told her stories about his childhood that I had never heard. His mother, she began, and then interrupted herself, as she would do often, saying Do you already know this? But my father's past had always been opaque to me, he spoke of it so seldom and it seemed so complex, a tangle of half brothers and cousins, too many to track. And he didn't speak to most of them; Bad blood, he would say whenever their names came up, cutting off any conversation. Do you know how young she was, my sister said, when our father was born she was still just a kid, only fourteen, can you imagine? When our father started school they rode the bus together, she for her final year and he for his first. There were other children too, three sons, and a daughter who died, none of them by the same father. She was a scandal, my sister said, can you imagine what it must have been like for her in that place? I couldn't reconcile what G. said with the small woman I had known, always at a remove, who seemed so proper and content when we visited her once a year or so in the house she shared with a man I thought of as my grandfather, though I guess I knew he wasn't, or not by blood, since my father only ever called him by his first name. My sister was right, she must have been a scandal in that town, and to her parents something worse than a scandal. They were the ones who took care of my father, especially his grandmother, who alone among his relations was spared his future scorn. He always called her Ma, the single syllable, and even now I have no other name for the woman I remember seeing only once, slight to the point of disappearance, with her beautiful white hair spread about her on the sheets in whatever hospital or facility she had been taken to to die in. I don't remember what time of year it was, or how far we had traveled, or why I was alone with my father, who lifted me up to set me gingerly on the bed next to that woman who was impossibly old, older than anyone I had ever seen, and whose image, though so much else is lost, remains vivid to me as day. My father sat on the other side and fed her like a child, spooning food from a dish; he murmured words of encouragement or recrimination when she rejected the food, sealing her lips against it or spitting it back into the bowl. I hadn't thought of her for years, the woman whose image returned to me so clearly, though my father spoke of her sometimes after she died, as he never spoke of his grandfather, who had died before I was born. Or never spoke of him to me, I should say, since my sister did know about him, and that night she told us what she knew. He was a hard man, my sister said, he tried to rein in his daughter, to discipline her and (perhaps he thought) to save her, and his

violence, provoked and unprovoked, governed my father's
life. But then they were a constant provocation, his daughter and her multiplying sons, her string of men and the children they left; it must have made them the talk of the
county, that bilious joyful talk of small places with little
news. He terrorized them, my sister said, his daughter and
her children, he threatened them, he beat them, he promised worse than beatings. Our father's father was older than
our grandmother, in his twenties when they met, and she had
fallen in love with him; if she took up with other men as a
way of defying her father, the first man wasn't just that, G.
said, she loved him, and the man loved her too. She was too
young to be going with men, she knew her father would be
angry, but she was in love, she slept with him, and then she
was pregnant with my father. He killed him, my sister said
then, before our father was born he killed him, and though
to that point we had been silent my other sister and I both
started at this, expressing our shock and disbelief. The
story G. told us then was disjointed, handed down incomplete: it was winter when his grandfather understood what
had happened, my sister said, there was a storm and he went
out into the storm to find the man who had ruined his daughter, as he must have thought of it; and he killed the man—
But how, I asked, interrupting her, and my sister couldn't
say, she only knew that he was found the next day frozen in
his car. But that's crazy, I blurted out, even in that place
how could such things happen, or happen without consequences? And anyway our father loved to tell stories, I went
on, he was always claiming outlandish things were true;
surely this was one of his Southern Gothics, I said. But my
sister insisted, something in how he told it convinced her it
was true, or that he believed it was true. And after all, I
thought, his belief was what mattered, and I wondered
when he had been given this account of his father, of the

absence of his father, whether he was still a child, and I wondered too how the absence had weighed on him, how he had explained it to himself until then. I wanted to know who had told him and why, whether his mother to make him angry or his grandfather to make him afraid. Besides, my sister said, it explains what happened to her, to my father's mother, she meant, who seemed to seek out not just other men but the least acceptable men, as if she gave herself to them not just to defy her father but to injure him, and increasingly to injure herself. Often they were violent men, my sister said, repeating what she had been told; from as early as he could remember my father was scared of them, and he was frightened of his grandfather, too, who lashed out at him and his brothers without warning. And they fought with one another, as kids and as adults, these boys with different fathers; one of them died a soldier before I was born and we hardly knew the others, we saw them so seldom. Two or three times when I was very young my father took us to a reunion, and each time there was a fight, a quick flare of violence that left one or more of them in the dirt. When they were children they felt no loyalty to one another, my father and his brothers; they shifted their allegiances whenever it suited, teaming up against one and then another, or making friends with one or another of the men who appeared as if from nowhere and never stayed for long. Most of all they courted their grandfather, whom they hated but needed, too, especially as their mother sought out more and more brutal men. It was like she wanted to be hurt by them, my sister said, and didn't care what happened to her sons. One day, she went on, when our father was still a boy, maybe eight or nine, he heard his mother shouting and ran to find her standing with one of his brothers in a field. In front of them was the boy's father, who was enraged past all restraint, my father realized; he wasn't surprised when he struck their mother, first with his open hand and then with his fist. And not just the woman, he struck the child too, not once or twice but many times, with a ferocity that frightened my father, who ran for help to the garage where his grandfather was working, bent over the hood of their car. And the child who was my father yelled at him to come, that the man was hurting his mother and his brother, that he (my father) was frightened, and his grandfather grabbed one of the tools around him, a heavy wrench, my sister said, and set off to the field and approached the man and brought the wrench down on him, beating the man who had been beating his daughter, not furiously but with an eerie calm, repeatedly, as his daughter cried for him to stop and my father felt a different fear. So did he kill him too, my other sister asked, but G. couldn't answer us; like all of her stories this one was patchworked and incomplete. But she did know that my father's grandfather bore a mark from that day, that the palm of his hand was welted and scarred where he had gripped the wrench, which had been resting on the engine and was red-hot, she said. It didn't even slow him down, she went on, can you imagine, for the rest of his life he was disfigured, the fingers on that hand were always a little bit curled, he couldn't open them all the way. But when he grabbed it it didn't even slow him down, he just took it in his hand like this—and here she raised her own hand, lifting it with her palm up and her fingers curled around an imaginary wrench, turning her wrist slightly as if it were dragged down by the weight of it. And though nothing in her story had been familiar to me I felt a sudden vertigo at the sight of it; I could see my father making that gesture, the very same, and I knew I must have heard the story before, that he must have told it to me when I was a child. It was my story too, I realized as my sister went on, and I wondered how much else I had forgotten about my father, how much I might still remember, how much was totally lost. As I sat by the water in Mladost, I held two images of my father in mind, weighing them against what I felt: in one he was a child, vulnerable and finally blameless as all children are blameless, and in the other he was old and in need and trying to repair what he had broken. I wanted to know what they could make me feel, these images, whether I could go to him as he had asked; but of all the images of that day these struck with the least force, my father as a child and my father dying, they struck with almost no force at all. I couldn't hold on to them, they slipped away as I remembered instead another image of my father, from the time after K. put an end to our friendship, when my father, too, finally broke with me. It was the end of a long series of events in that large house where the atmosphere had become unbearable; my father and I hardly spoke to each other, maybe both of us afraid of what we might say. He was gone more often, he stayed later at work and took more trips away, on whatever pretext heading to Chicago or New York, leaving my stepmother with me and the older of my sisters, who was still just a toddler. I can see now how unhappy my stepmother was, how often my father abandoned her and how trapped she must have felt, and I can see that if she and I fought it was because for both of us the other was a safer target than my father. We attacked each other for the slightest reason, for no reason at all, raising our voices and slamming doors; and one night, after a particularly vicious argument, when I had crossed a line the nature of which I no longer remember, my stepmother ordered me out of the house. She locked the door leading from the basement stairs, ensuring that at some point I would have to leave, which I did quickly, without waiting her out, escaping as I always did through the garage. I was angry as I walked the two or so miles to my mother's house, but I was satisfied, too; they punished me all the time but they had never kicked me out, and whatever I had done it didn't warrant that. I thought my father would agree with me, I was sure he would tell my stepmother to let me back in. I walked quickly, eager to get to my mother's house and call him; he was in New York, I had the number of the hotel where he always stayed. I visited my mother most weekends but I didn't often show up unannounced, so she knew something must be wrong when she opened the door. She asked me what had happened but I didn't answer. I need to call my father, I said, which was how we always referred to him in that house, my mother never called him by name. I dropped my bag by the door (I had brought my schoolbooks with me, a few overnight things) and went to the kitchen where the phone hung on the wall. My mother could see I was upset, she followed me and asked me again what was wrong, Tell me before you call him, she said, you need to calm down. But I didn't want to calm down, I liked the indignation I felt and that I thought my father would share, I wanted to call him while it was still hot. I imagined him comforting me, telling me he would make things right, as he used to take it upon himself as a matter of course to do. But this confidence disappeared the instant he picked up, which he did too quickly, on the first ring. He was waiting for me to call, which meant that my stepmother had already spoken with him, and by the tone in his voice I knew he was convinced of her side of things. I couldn't expect any sympathy, he would make me apologize to her, I would have to apologize again and again until she was satisfied; it would be humiliating, I thought, and she would love it. I prepared for it as I began to tell my father how outrageously she had acted, It's where I live, I said to him, she can't just kick me out. I went on for some time and he listened without saying a word, so that I might almost have thought the line had been cut except that I could sense his presence so clearly. His silence made me feel I was being led somewhere other than I intended, as if I were digging my own grave; and so I stopped short and waited for him to speak, leaning into his silence. I waited for what seemed like a long time, until finally I spoke again. Tell her to let me back in the house, I said to my father, and if I used the imperative I spoke with a tone of defeat. I knew I was waiting for admonishment, but I took it for granted that once I had apologized enough they would let me back in; it was my home, and in the world I came from children weren't simply turned out. Tell her to let me back in, I said, and here my father did make a sound. I heard him shifting his weight in his chair, and then he exhaled, it wasn't quite a sigh, it wasn't angry or sad but emotionless, and he spoke for the first time since his greeting. If, he said, staying just a moment longer the sentence he would pronounce, if what you say about yourself is true, you're not welcome in my house. It was my turn to be silent now, at first because I didn't understand what he meant, and then because I did. I had a sense of something beginning, of a great weight dislodged and moving in the single direction it could. What are you talking about, I said finally, and my father answered, he told me that they had found, my stepmother and he, a notebook in my room. I knew the notebook he meant, a journal I had started keeping not long before, in which I had written about K. and what I had felt in his room, what I had learned about myself there. I had been careful to hide the journal; if they had come across it it was because they had searched, though my father gave no account or explanation of this. They had found it and seen what I had written, he said simply, they had read it weeks ago. What they learned about me had brought the two of them together, I realized, they were a united front, and I imagined they had spent weeks plotting how best to use what they knew. I was sure it was my stepmother who had searched my room, my father would never have bothered, and as he spoke I realized how entirely I had played into her hand. Is it true, he asked when he had finished speaking, giving me a choice, or the semblance of a choice. He presented it to me as if it were something that might be spoken away and made right, but I couldn't speak it away, I realized; to speak it away would have been to speak myself away, what else could it have meant, and so Yes, I said, laying claim to myself, it is true, yes. My father exhaled again, sharply this time, so that even before he spoke I flinched, and I could see my mother stiffen as she watched me, standing at the sink with a cigarette in her hand. My father spoke in a different tone now, almost with a different voice, the voice of his own childhood, I thought, thick with the dirt he usually worked so hard to conceal. So you like the little boys, that voice said, the voice almost of instinct, the voice of the look he had given me once and of what had once fouled the air. As young as I was, I knew what he said was absurd, I was myself a little boy, what could he be accusing me of, though now I think it was his only understanding of what I could be, the person I was was lost in it. But it didn't matter that it was absurd, I was already crying, I was a mess of tears, and when my mother started to come toward me I motioned her away, turning my back to her. I was ashamed of my tears, I could hardly breathe, and it was all I could do to say to him But I'm your son, which was my only appeal and the last thing I would say. He made a dismissive sound, almost a laugh, and then he spoke again, with a snarling voice I had never heard before, he said The hell you are. He went on, he spoke without stopping, A faggot, he said, if I had known you would never have been born. You disgust me, he said, do you know that, you disgust me, how could you be my son? As I listened to him say these things it was as though even as I laid claim to myself I found there was nothing to claim, nothing or next to nothing, as though I were dissolving and my tears were the outward sign of that dissolution. He was still speaking, there were still things he wanted to say, but I hung the phone back on the wall, holding it there a moment as if to clutch at something, as my mother crossed the room and put her hand on my back. I laid my head against the wall, hiding my face from her. I was still crying, but more than shock or grief I felt anger, more than anger, I was enraged, and rage filled me up with something that would not dissolve. What would I be without the anger I felt then, I wondered as I stood looking over the water, the anger I still feel, it ebbs or surges but is always there; whatever it has kept me from, without it I would have lost myself altogether. I lifted my hand. After so much time it was an effort to release my grip on the wadded page that was barely more than pulp now, but I let it fall into the stream and watched the water carry it away. I wouldn't answer, I wouldn't see my father again, I wouldn't mourn him or pour earth on him. I stood watching the water for some time, I'm not sure how long, until I was startled by a distant noise that made its way over the sound of the water. It was an unmusical clanging that it took me a moment to recognize as a bell, a large bell as if from a tower, though I didn't know of any such towers in Mladost, which was built by the Communists and so built free of churches; even now the only places of worship are little clapboard affairs, American missionaries in rented halls. I didn't know of anything in Mladost that could make this sound, grand and unlovely, a single bell, ringing twice in quick succession with each pull of the rope (I imagined), so that its lopsided toll rolled out over the water and the trees. I walked toward it, and soon I could feel the ground getting smoother, becoming a path that led upward, until finally the uneven stones became brick. It was a lovely path, immaculate as few things are here, and on the right there was a low stone wall that as the path mounted joined with another wall, plaster and brilliantly white. It was a compound of some sort, tucked here behind the *blokove*, something large and old, I thought, though it was perfectly maintained; the bricks in the path were old, as were the trees that overhung them. I followed the sound, the bell ringing quite close now from the other side of the wall, as the path widened until it was large enough for a car, and I realized it must extend all the way up to the road. There was a gate in the wall, two large wooden wings interrupting the stone. It was closed, but in each of these doors there was an opening in the shape of a cross, and as the ringing of the bell stopped, I peered through at the grounds within, a series of small buildings and paths through green spaces. It was a community, not a church but a monastery, which predated the district and must have been built when the neighborhood was nothing but countryside, when Sofia must have seemed at once accessible and comfortably far away. I had heard a summons for prayer, then, though I saw no movement within. There are monasteries all over the country, in most of which a single monk keeps watch, or two, they're dying out here like everywhere else; but there was still someone ringing a summons for prayer, even if no one was around to answer it. I set off again, intending to follow the path up to the road and then to find my way home. I had decided not to go back to school, I would go straight home, but after another turn in the path I stopped again. There was a clearing to the left and at the side of the path a horse was grazing, still hitched to its cart. Horses are common in Mladost, gypsies use them on their rounds, but I had never seen one unattended before. There was no one in sight; maybe someone had been called by the summons after all. It was a pitiful creature, sickly and thin, its skin hanging loose over protruding ribs; it might have been a portrait of misery, I thought as I stepped closer, but it was grazing sedately enough, pulling at the sparse tufts of grass in the rocky soil. I watched it for a few minutes, and then I laid my hand on its flank, which was dark and broiling with sun, almost too hot to touch. I felt it give a sudden sigh, a quick unburdening of breath as it shifted its frame a little. It wasn't tied up, I saw, it could have wandered off anytime it chose; but there was nowhere for it to go, of course, and the cart I supposed was heavy, and there was something however meager to be had there where it stood.

III

POX

When the knock came, quick and assured, I heard it without surprise, my hand steady at the stove where I was warming the simple meal I had made. It wasn't late, despite the darkness beyond the windows at my back; it was February, the dark came early, and what had been an unnervingly mild season had turned sharp and bitter, the coldest winter on record, with a fierce wind that burned whatever skin one left uncovered. He hadn't pressed the buzzer from the street below, which would have given me some warning and a moment to prepare; he must have thought surprise would be to his advantage, I thought, and I imagined him waiting for someone to come in or out of the building's locked front door, sheltering as best he could against the wind, a cigarette tight at his lips. There was no need for any of it; I would have buzzed him in as quickly as I opened my apartment door, which I unlatched without even drawing aside the little cover of the peephole, though I did pause briefly with my hand on the knob, drawing a steadying breath. It was almost two years to the day since I had last seen Mitko. When I returned from Varna I did everything I could to ensure I wouldn't see him again; I blocked him on Facebook and Skype, I scrubbed him from my e-mail and phone.

These were measures against myself, really, I wanted to make it more difficult for me to find him in a spasm of remorse; and though I thought of him often, though he appeared in dreams from which I woke more excited than I was by anything in my waking life, I didn't regret what I had done. I had missed him, but more than missing him I had been relieved that he was gone.

The corridor was dark when I opened the door. The light was set to a timer, which must have run out since he pressed the switch at the bottom of the stairs, if he had; or maybe he thought darkness, too, was to his advantage. I could only see him thanks to the light from my own apartment, which barely reached him where he leaned against the opposite wall, as though he had waited a long time for me to answer, or been prepared to wait. He straightened up, coming farther into the light, and I could see he wasn't dressed at all for the cold; he was wearing a thin jacket and torn jeans, and his canvas shoes were soaked through. He was unshaved and unkempt, thinner than he had been, though he had always been thin; it was as if he had been worn away somehow in the months since I had seen him. He stood with his shoulders slumped, his hands—which I remembered in constant motion, always seeking some occupation—shoved firmly in his pockets. *Dobur vecher*, he said, a formal greeting, as if he were unsure of his footing, and I repeated it back to him in the same tone. But I wasn't unhappy to see him. Something in me leapt up at the sight of him, despite his state and my desire to keep a tight rein on my feeling.

We stood for a moment looking at each other (what did he see, I wondered, what tale of the two years did the sight of me tell?), and then he jerked his head up a little, indicating the apartment behind me. *Mozhe li*, he said, may I, and I drew back from the entrance and motioned him in, saying

Yes, of course, *zapovyadaite*, come in. I realized too late that I had used the polite form of the verb, so that my invitation at once welcomed him and held him off. He stepped forward, only now reaching out his hand, and his grip was as I remembered it, strong and cordial, though he didn't meet my eye with the eager and disarming look I remembered from our first meeting. He looked down at our hands instead, his brown against mine, the ends of his fingers broad and blunt, almost square, and then he bent to unlace his shoes and I took in his smell, wet and unwashed and stinking of alcohol. I followed him into the room, where nothing had changed, the bare table was still by the window, the shabby sofa along the wall, with a street map of Sofia pinned above it. When he glanced at the stove he said I'm sorry, you were having dinner, I'm interrupting, and I looked at him curiously, surprised by a brittle formality I had never seen in him before. What did he think I was feeling, I wondered, that would be pleased or appeased by this; or maybe it was something else, an attempt at dignity, at shoring himself up against whatever had worn him so roughly and brought him finally to my door.

He stood in the center of the room with his arms crossed, his hands clamped beneath them, and he was swaying back and forth, whether out of nervousness or a need for warmth I wasn't sure. I haven't seen you for a long time, I said finally, lamely, how are you, and at this he did look up, but briefly and without fully lifting his head, so that it was as if from below that he met my eyes. I'm not good, he said, and then more firmly, I'm bad, I need to talk to you, I've come to tell you something. Lots of people wouldn't come, he said, they'd say he's an American, let him worry about himself, but I'm not like them. What are you talking about, I asked, what's going on, feeling at once exasperation and dread of what was to come. And then I lost track of what he said, he

spoke too quickly or unclearly, so that even when he repeated himself I was lost; though I knew the words I couldn't
make any real sense of them, and I turned my palms up in
defeat. I could see his frustration; it had been hard for him
to say whatever he was telling me, I felt, it was as though he
had overcome something to say it, and having succeeded it
was intolerable to have finally said nothing at all. He sat down
on the sofa, spreading his legs wide, and leaned forward to
open up the laptop I had left lying on the coffee table. I'll
write it, he said, motioning for me to sit beside him, which
I did, excited to be near him though I didn't intend to touch
him, though I intended whatever the provocation to resist.

The Internet browser was open when the screen lit up,
and Mitko began to type directly into the navigation bar,
the single line of text stretching out across it. He was a slow
typist, using just one finger of each hand, using too the codes
and abbreviations of chat room transliteration, which had
only slowly over my years here become legible to me. But
I understood his story well enough now, and my disquiet
deepened as I shook my head from left to right in affirmation when he paused, as he did every few words, to ask
Razbirash li? A few days ago, I read, he had begun to have a
problem, it had never happened before, he felt a pain in his
groin and there was a white discharge from his penis. As
he typed it occurred to me, oddly and inappropriately, that
he used the same word, *teche*, one might use for a dripping
faucet, and I filed it away, this detail of usage, a distraction
from the dread I felt. Okay, I said, since he had paused, waiting to make sure I had caught up, did you to go a doctor, and
he nodded, bending over the keyboard again, writing that he
had gone to a clinic and had blood drawn and been told that
he had syphilis. Oh, I said, drawing back without thinking,
a reflex against contagion and against the word, too, feeling
horror at a nineteenth-century disease I only knew about

from books, so that my first thought, immediate and vivid, was of Flaubert on his travels, some account I had read of his climbing down from horse or camel to change bandages that had been soaked through.

Mitko must have taken my recoil for disbelief, since he said sharply Do you think I'm lying, and then stood up. I believe you, I said quickly, seeing his hand at his waist, of course I believe you, that's not necessary, but he had already undone his belt, and, fumbling just a moment with the safety pin that held the flaps of denim together (both the button and the zipper gone), with one swift motion he lowered both his jeans and his briefs to his knees. I was amazed again by how casual he could be in these moments, how little such exposure meant to him, and I couldn't help but look at his cock, which I had known so well and which was the same, heavy and long, without any signs of disease; I was taken aback by my eagerness to see it. Mitko took it in one hand and pinched the base with two fingers, pulling them slowly up the length of it. It was the gesture I remembered as the final act of sex, milking the last of a desired substance, and I watched as a single drop emerged at the tip, cloudy and white, indistinguishable from semen, really, and maybe it was the very similarity that so repulsed me, that turned my stomach as Mitko used the forefinger of his other hand to gather the discharge that was so much like a pearl, even in my disgust it was the unavoidable comparison. He gave his own look of revulsion; *Gadno*, he said, disgusting. He held his contaminated hands away from himself and walked awkwardly to the bathroom, his cock dangling, his jeans still around his knees, his briefs, I noticed now, stained a brownish off-white at the front, as if he suffered from a kind of chronic incontinence, as I suppose he did. It must be terrible, I thought, remembering his fastidiousness, to find oneself a source of such pollution, to have it flow out unchecked.

He took his time in the bathroom, washing his hands and then rising on his toes and leaning forward to place the tip of his penis in the flow of water. I watched him, still sitting on the couch, as he dried himself with toilet paper and then pulled his briefs back up, holding the stained cloth away from his skin as long as he could before he let it snap back into place.

He returned to the main room and sat down again beside me. That's serious, I said, I'm sorry, and he shook his head in agreement. Then he looked at me. Have you had any problems, he asked, anything like this? Me, I said, taken aback, of course not, no, nothing at all. At the clinic, he went on, they said I've had it for a long time, that's what I came to tell you. You need to get checked, he said, and I nodded in consent. All right, I said, I will. I wasn't very worried: it had been two years, and I hadn't noticed anything to cause alarm, certainly nothing so dramatic as Mitko's own symptoms. But it was also true that I hadn't been tested for anything in years. The terror I had felt constantly when I was younger had given way to something like carelessness, which I knew was irresponsible, though I mostly took the usual precautions, and anyway it was an easy enough thought to avoid. Lots of guys wouldn't have told you, Mitko said again, they would have said what do I owe him, he can fuck himself. But I'm not like that, he went on, and you're my friend. I've never stopped thinking of you as my friend, he said, shifting the pitch of the conversation just slightly, making it more intimate. This too was a different tone, one I hadn't heard from him before, retrospective, almost regretful, though I didn't really trust it, I doubted it was his conscience alone that had brought him back to me. Are you sorry, he said then, deepening this tone still further, are you sorry that you came to Varna that time? I didn't answer at first, remembering how frightened I had been that night, and thinking too of the whole false history between us, falser now that I've turned it over so often. No, I said, I don't regret it, and as I said it it was true. And you, I said, and he drew his head up in a single quick jerk, not quite a nod, *Ne, ne suzhalyavam.* For the first time since he had arrived he smiled, not the eager smile I remembered from before but something that lightened the mood. *Radvam se*, he said, I'm glad you're not sorry, and then he placed his hand on my knee, not meaning it as a seduction exactly, the fact of his illness dismissed any thought of it, but as a re-establishment of contact, I thought, a suggestion that at some point we might begin again what we had halted. Mitko, I said, I should tell you, I have a friend now, and I paused, not sure how to clarify what I meant, the Bulgarian word allowing for so many possibilities; *imam postoyanen priyatel*, I said finally, a constant friend, the awkward phrase the best I could manage. I wanted to make things clear, to draw firm lines, but I realized even as I spoke I was taking for granted the fact that Mitko would come again to my door, that almost certainly I would let him in. Is he Bulgarian, Mitko asked, catching my meaning, and I said he wasn't; we met here, I said, but he's Portuguese, he lives in Lisbon, and then I stopped, feeling I shouldn't say more. I wanted to keep my relationship with R. to myself, and the thought of him gave new urgency to Mitko's warning. How would I forgive myself if I had infected him, if I had dragged him into the world from which (as I thought of it) he had lifted me out?

Yasno, Mitko said, drawing back his hand, I get it; he seemed happy to let the subject drop. I had noticed his eyes flick once or twice, as if involuntarily, toward the pan still lying by the stove, and I stood and relit the burner, asking him if he was hungry. It wasn't really a question, and he didn't pretend to consider it. While the food was warming he turned back to my laptop, logging on to Facebook and,

I was sure, the Bulgarian hookup site I remembered from before, and then he closed the computer and sat with me at the little table. I was surprised that I couldn't remember our ever having shared a meal before in that way, quietly and seated and alone. We didn't talk at first; Mitko dug into the food and I watched him eat, surprised by how happy I was to have him there. I wondered how much this feeling owed to him, to his company or the pleasure he took in the poor meal I had made, and how much it depended on some gratified notion of myself, my willingness to set aside the past and a generosity I knew he would call on before he left, which was real generosity now, I thought, since I would ask nothing in return for it. He looked up and smiled when he caught me watching him, and I smiled back. I asked him how he had passed the last two years, whether he had been in Varna, whether he had found work. He looked at me, briefly silent, and then, For a while I was in a bad place, he said and paused, as if unsure how to continue, or as if waiting for me to draw him out. What do you mean, I asked, what kind of place, and he set down his fork, which he had been holding in the palm of his hand like a child, all five fingers circled around the handle. I did some bad things, he said, and I was caught, and they put me away for a year. In prison, I asked stupidly, what else could it be, and he wagged his head yes. What did you do, I asked, remembering of course our scene in Varna, the face he had shown that seemed capable of so much, and that was so different from the face I looked at now.

Mitko made a dismissive gesture with his shoulders, shrugging as he picked up his fork again. It was a job, he said, I worked for a guy in Varna. He helps people, he gives them money, if you need something you can go to him. But you can't just take somebody's money, he said, almost as if I had challenged him, you have to pay it back. And if somebody didn't pay it back, he would send us. You would hurt them, I said, and he shrugged again. *Malko*, a little, but never too badly, and then, as if affronted, I never hurt anyone badly, I'm not that kind of person, there are people who do that but not me. He lowered his fork to his plate and pushed his food around a bit. And then, Mitko went on, if they still didn't pay, we would go where they lived and take everything, and here he gestured around the room, as if imagining it stripped bare, the television, the computer, the furniture, we'd take all of it, he wouldn't have anything left. But that's normal, he said, again as if defending the justice of it, you can't take somebody's money and not pay it back. I didn't challenge this statement or agree with it, I watched him without saying a word. And that's it, he said, I had worked for him before, on and off, but this time I got in trouble, I had to go away. It wasn't nice there, it's a bad place, I won't tell you what it was like. But I'm done with that now, he said, making a gesture as if wiping his hands clean, I don't want to do that anymore.

What happened when you got out, I asked, what did you do then? He shrugged again, I was in Sofia for a while, he said, I found some work here, and he told me how he had worked on a construction site, not as a builder but as security, watching over the premises at night. *Skuchna rabota*, he said, boring work. I thought about calling you, I still had your number, but I wasn't sure you would want me to, I thought you were still mad. I shrugged, wondering if I was, and he went on, I worked there a few months, and then it stopped. At my inquisitive glance, They ran out of money, he said, it's what always happens, we had to stop working. He had gone back to Varna to his mother's apartment, which was all right in the summer, when there were people, he said, there was something to do, and I thought how he must love it, those few weeks when his city became a little Europe, the beautiful young coming from the west for the cheap beaches and beer, the Balkan carnival, maybe it seemed like the life that should have been his. But no one's there now, he said, the city's empty, and so he had come back to Sofia to look for work. But there isn't any work, he said, what can you do. I stayed with friends for a while, but there's no one you can count on here, and now his face darkened, the people who say they are your friends aren't friends at all. And then this happened, he said, gesturing down at his lap, and I don't have any money; they want me to take pills first, and then if they don't work I need an injection. But the pills are forty leva, he said, and then, disingenuously, where will I get forty leva? I'll help you, I said, of course, don't worry. We had finished eating already, and so I stood and took my wallet from the little shelf by the door, taking out forty leva and then another twenty. Here, I said, for the medicine. *Shte se opravish*, I said, you'll get better, and he took the money and thanked me, for the food and for my help, he said, taking my hand in his. I wanted to ask him where he would go, if he had a place to spend the night, but I was afraid he might press me to extend my generosity further than it would reach. At the door he knelt to put on his shoes, which were still damp, and drew on his thin jacket, and then he stood and opened the door, the corridor dark behind him. Thank you again, he said, and then, so quickly that I didn't have a chance to stop him, even if I had wanted to, he placed both of his hands on my shoulders and leaned toward me, touching his lips to my cheek. He leaned back again and smiled, withdrawing his hands, but not before tousling my hair, smiling now with the unguardedness I remembered. It was a friendly gesture, unromantic, which didn't dismiss the intimacy of his kiss but set it in a new key, and I was filled with fondness as he stepped out and pulled the door shut behind him. There was no temptation, I thought, there was no danger of his upsetting the new balance I had found, the monogamy that still had the novelty of a break from long habit. After I turned the key in its lock I stood with my hand on the door, not with the thought of opening it again but just to listen to him make his way down the hall. He had already gone down the stairs before I remembered to press the switch for the hallway light, setting the timer running though it was already past its use.

I hardly slept that night. Almost as soon as Mitko left I started to worry, and I lay in bed wondering what I would tell R. if the tests came back positive, as now I was sure they would. I had written him an e-mail, saying I was too busy to talk on Skype, as we usually did every night before going to sleep. I didn't tell him about Mitko's visit. It wasn't my intention to lie, and R. already knew about Mitko, like everything else in my past he was part of the story that had led us to each other; it's a way of being in love, I think, to see the past like that. R. would worry even more than I did, I thought, it was better to spare him until I was sure. The next day was a Friday, and I had the first two periods of the morning free. I had never been ill in my three years in Sofia, or never ill enough to seek out care; I don't like going to doctors' offices, I've hated them since I was a child, with their humiliations, their assaults on necessary privacies. But there was a clinic near my school, in a glass-fronted building situated right at the turn from Malinov Boulevard to the private road leading to the police academy and the American College. I walked past this clinic every day, and I knew it was where the other teachers went, that it was modern and efficient and that someone there would speak

English. This was important, as I realized I lacked the vocabulary to request the tests I needed or explain the circumstances of my case, and I imagined how my helplessness in the language would compound the helplessness of illness. I was reassured, as I opened the door to the clinic, by a waiting room that wouldn't have been terribly out of place in America. There were a number of women bustling behind the long counter in the aggressively heated room, which was already full, even though I had arrived shortly after they opened. I was nervous as I entered, and annoyed with myself for being nervous. For all its literary horror I knew syphilis was easily treated, I would only need antibiotics, probably a single shot. It was stupid to be embarrassed, I said to myself, it was an infection like any other. But as I stepped up to the counter none of this eased what I felt, which was strong and deep-seated, part of that larger shame of which my whole story with Mitko, from our first encounter to this deferred consequence, was merely the latest iteration.

One of the women looked up, her fingers pausing at the keyboard, and my tension was relieved by a brightness of welcome I had grown unaccustomed to. She looked at me expectantly, waiting for me to speak, and when I asked in Bulgarian if she spoke English she seemed genuinely sorry that she didn't, no, not a word. She turned to the other women behind the desk, all of whom confessed a similar helplessness. Wait just a moment, she said, picking up the phone, we'll find someone, and as I stood I glanced around the waiting room, relieved that none of the eight or ten people sitting in the plastic chairs, none of them visibly ill, seemed to have paid us any mind. Here, the woman behind the desk said, standing now and leaning forward to point down a hallway lined with examination rooms, this woman can help you. I looked over to see a large and much older woman walking toward us, dressed in the formless uniform of an orderly or nurse, her thinning blond hair styled severely in a masculine cut. There was something severe in her face as well, for all its heavy roundness, a tightness about the lips suggesting not just a difficult morning but a more fundamental fatigue. Good morning, she said, a plummy British accent coming through the Balkan, what can we do for you today? She spoke more loudly than necessary, showing off her English, as people often do here, where the language when spoken well confers some prestige, and I realized I had already taken a dislike to her. Yes, I said, speaking not quite furtively but at a much lower volume, I would like to get a full set of tests, and then I paused, realizing I wasn't sure of the words even in English, a full screening, I said finally, for STDs, thinking then that maybe the acronym would be lost on her, that I should have spoken the words in full. But she understood immediately, saying Yes, of course, and she leaned over the counter, resting her large breasts on its surface, to reach for a sheet of paper. All right, she said, drawing a pen from her pocket, let's see, and then she began reading off the tests, still in a loud voice as she circled them, saying So, you will want HIV, pronouncing it as a single syllable, *hiff,* and gonorrhea, chlamydia, hepatitis, and then, moving the pen down the page, anything else? Well, I said, yes, but she clucked her tongue before I could go on, having come across the word at the bottom of the page, Yes, of course, syphilis, speaking all along in the same inflated tone, either clueless or malicious, I thought. Several people were looking at us now, including one very beautiful man about my age, whose eyes caught mine before I quickly looked away. No one needed English to understand, since the names she circled were the same in both languages, and I hardened my features against the curiosity we were attracting. So, she said, handing me the page, come along, and I followed her

down the long hallway, relieved to escape scrutiny and trying not to glance through the open doors of the examination
rooms we passed. We turned left at the end of the corridor,
stopping outside a closed door marked *Laboratoriya*. Please,
sit, she said, motioning me toward the short bench against
the wall, and then she took the page she had just given me
and let herself into the room, closing the door behind her.
She opened it again a moment later, saying All right, I will
leave you now, they will let you in in a moment. If you
need anything, just ask for me, she said, taking her leave as
I thanked her, though after she left I realized she had never
told me her name.

About twenty minutes had passed, and I had started to
worry about making it to my class on time, when the door
opened and a woman ushered me in. *Dobur den*, I said,
nodding at her, and she pointed to the large chair in the corner, telling me to sit. The room was full of instruments and
machines, many of them working away, and the surfaces
were crowded with trays of red vials arranged meticulously
in rows. She was working at one of these trays, wrapping an
adhesive label around a vial before sliding it into place.
Sega, she said, now, as she turned toward me and took from
a table what I assumed was the page specifying my tests.
She studied it briefly and then took a number of empty vials,
a dismaying number, of different sizes gathered from various
trays. She arranged them on the little table to my right and
then sat on a stool beside me. Now, she said again, looking
at me for the first time, are we going to have any problems?
I looked at her uncomprehendingly and she went on, Will
you be all right, will you be—and she used the word *muzhki*,
manly; people say it all the time here, *Druzh se muzhki*, act
like a man, and I always resented it when someone said it
to me, it felt like a challenge they weren't sure I could meet.
And anyway it was the kind of doctorly banter I hated most,

a chummy preliminary to unpleasantness. She looked much the same as my earlier guide, older and formless and with short, thinning hair, though hers had been dyed the alarming shade of red inexplicably popular in Sofia. I'll be fine, I said, pulling my arm from its sleeve, and then opening and closing my hand as she tied a rubber tourniquet around my bicep. I wasn't troubled by needles, but I hated the pressure of the tourniquet, the slow rising of my veins against the skin. Ah, the woman said in appreciation, here's a nice one, and she told me to squeeze hard as she quickly swabbed it with alcohol. I turned away then, as I always do, looking at the little square of window with its glimpse of sky, and then I closed my eyes as I felt the metal on my skin, the sharp prick and then the unsettling dull ache of the needle in the vein. She knew what she was doing, I thought, as she snapped the first tube in place with one hand and untwisted the tourniquet with the other, telling me at the same time to relax my grip; I had certainly had worse, though I was taken aback to notice, as I looked at my arm again, strangely alien to me now as it did its work, vigorously pumping blood, that she was doing all of this without gloves. She moved through her vials quickly, deftly corking and uncorking until finally she drew out the long spike, at the same time pressing a ball of cotton to the wound. Press here, she said, *zdravo*, hard, and then gathered the vials and took them to a table, where she began labeling them and placing them in trays. I didn't get up at first, waiting for instruction, and then, Am I finished, I asked, and she said *Da da* dismissively, busy with her work, telling me I could return for the results after lunch.

I made it to school in time for my class, disappointing the students who were gathered at the door, surprised to find it locked and excited at the prospect of a broken routine. There were only a few minutes before the second bell, no time for me to gather my thoughts, but they were good

kids, talkative, amiable, eager for debate, and though I kept
thinking about those vials even now giving up their secrets,
eventually I lost myself in the conversation's back and forth,
grateful that it was a day on which the machinery basically
worked. I taught four periods, two before and two after lunch,
and I was sorry to see the last of the students go, for once
I would happily have taken any offer to prolong our talk.
The same women were at the counter when I returned to
the clinic, and the one I had spoken to before picked up the
phone when she saw me, talking with someone quickly as I
approached. You speak some Bulgarian, yes, she asked, settling the phone back in its cradle, and then she told me that
my results weren't quite ready, inviting me to sit and wait, it
won't be long, she said. The waiting area was empty now,
and in general the clinic was quieter, free of the morning's
bustle. I sat in one of the plastic chairs beside a long, low
table covered with pamphlets, informational brochures on
eye care and diabetes, advertisements for medications, for a
particular brand of lubricant, the glossy paper swirled haphazardly about. I glanced at one brochure but could make
little of it, even the cover was full of words I didn't know,
though when I opened it the images were familiar from
other waiting rooms I had sat in, the stock visual language
of medical admonishment and reassurance. For all that I
avoided such offices these images, with their warnings about
precaution and prevention, had long been part of my most
private sense of myself. I grew up at the height of the AIDS
panic, when desire and disease seemed essentially bound together, the relationship between them not something that
could be managed but absolute and unchangeable, a consequence and its cause. Disease was the only story anyone ever
told about men like me where I was from, and it flattened
my life to a morality tale, in which I could be either chaste
or condemned. Maybe that's why, when I finally did have

sex, it wasn't so much pleasure I sought as the exhilaration of setting aside restraint, of pretending not to be afraid, a thrill of release so intense it was almost suicidal. As I sat flipping through brochures, waiting for someone to collect and usher me elsewhere, I remembered the first time I was tested, in my last year of high school, at a free clinic in Michigan. I had left my hometown two years before, and in that time news had reached me of friends falling ill. I knew I must have been exposed to it, I had been extravagantly reckless; and as I waited for the nurse to call my name, two weeks after the test, I was sure of the news she would bring. My best friend was beside me, and I held his hand as the woman read me the results and I felt not relief, exactly, but disappointment, or something so bewilderingly mixed I still have no good name for it. Maybe it was just that I wanted the world to have a meaning, and that the meaning I wanted it to have was chastisement.

For the first time since I had arrived, the clinic door opened, and the nurse I had spoken with that morning came in. She was moving slowly, holding between two fingers of one hand a thin plastic cup of coffee, the bottom sagging, distended with heat. Hello, she said in her strange accent, are you here for your results, and when I told her that I had been waiting for some time, that I was beginning to feel forgotten, her face darkened in sympathy. Well, she said, let's see what we can do, and she turned and began speaking quickly to the receptionist. She referred to me as *gospodinut*, the gentleman, which surprised me; older people here usu-ally call me *momcheto*, the boy, a friendly term I like more. Come with me, she said, turning, and I followed her to the room she had taken me to before, a strange weightlessness in my abdomen. I'll be just a moment, she said, wait here, and then she knocked sharply on the laboratory door and opened it without waiting for an answer. She left the door ajar, and I could hear something of the conversation she had, or at least her voice, which was louder than the other and tinged with something like rebuke. I heard a chair groan as someone rose from it, and then a quieter, extended exchange I could make little of, though I knew it must mean they had something to discuss, and I realized, with a sharp clenching in the pit of my stomach, that I was surprised, that for all my anxiety I hadn't really believed I had it, and I thought of R., of what I would have to tell him and of how he would respond.

The voices drew closer and I heard the technician say Do we just put it in his hand, and the other woman, my guide, saying Yes, of course, they are his results. She stepped into the hallway alone, holding the page and smiling, and perhaps it was only in my imagination that her smile seemed changed. Tell me, she said, have you ever had a positive result on any of these tests before, and I said no, I hadn't, I had always been negative. Well, she said, there may be a problem, and she held up the sheet in her hand for me to see. Here, she said, pointing to a line where there was a mark handwritten in ink, a plus sign or cross, surrounded by Cyrillic letters and other symbols she didn't give me a chance to decipher. You have tested positive for syphilis, she said. Since it was the news I had prepared myself for I didn't react, which seemed to surprise or disappoint her, as if she had been cheated of an intended effect. It's a very serious infection, she said, almost sternly, as though I were a child she had to school. Yes, I said meekly, of course, and she went on, mollified, But this is only a first test, you must have another to confirm it. Can we do that now, I asked, sick at the thought of more waiting, but she said Oh no, as if surprised by the question, you have to go to another clinic for that, we can't do it here. But here, she said, pulling out a smaller piece of paper that she had been holding behind the report of my

results, I've written it down for you, where you need to go.
THE XXIX POLYCLINIC, she had written, the numbers in block
Roman numerals, and beneath it GOTSE DELCHEV, the name
of a district where I had never been. As I took this paper, I
imagined having to find my way to an unfamiliar part of
the city, to a public clinic where no one would speak English, and I thought of all I had heard about such places, the
long lines and poor facilities, the incompetence or disregard
of doctors. She must have seen how I felt, and as if taking
pity, she said One of the buses that stops outside will take you
there, I think, I'm sorry I don't know which one. She started
walking toward the reception area again, having done
everything she could, and I followed obediently behind her.
That was why I hated clinics and examinations, I thought,
the indignity they inflict, the way they let doctors and nurses
deliver a sentence and then wash their hands of it, so that
however they change one's life they remain unchanged
themselves. You will have to go on Monday, she said, they
will be closing soon for the weekend. Tell me, I said, as we
neared the glass doors of the entrance, once I have the
results from the second test, can I get the treatment here? I
had spoken this in what must have been a hopeful tone, or
a tone of entreaty, and it seemed to me she replied with
pleasure as she opened the door for me and said again Oh no,
it's best that they take care of everything from there. I stepped
outside, and then half turned back to raise my hand in goodbye. But it was a wasted gesture; she had already moved on
to other tasks, letting the door swing shut behind her.

On Sunday night Mitko appeared again. He buzzed up from the street this time, confident I would answer; or maybe he had gotten tired of waiting for someone to open the door. It was late, I was already in bed with a book in my hand. It had been a long, anxious weekend, and I had hardly needed to exaggerate when I wrote to my department chair that I was too ill to come in, freeing the next day for the clinic. I was caught up again in the poetry of the illness, as it were, that aura or miasma of shame; I felt unclean, I wanted to hide myself away, feeling, for all I had learned of the disease, that even touching someone might contaminate them. I washed my hands compulsively, and made obsessive use of the little bottles of antiseptic gel that most teachers keep close by. I stayed at home as much as I could, and when I had to go out I shied away from any kind of contact, careful not to bump or nudge into people on the street or in the grocery store, which is difficult to avoid here, where there's such a different idea of personal space. I had been sick before, of course, but this felt like more than sickness, like a physical confirmation of shame.

I told R. everything on Friday night. I called him on Skype as soon as I saw him online; I had been waiting for a while, he had been out with friends and got home later than planned. He was still in his street clothes when his image filled my screen, his hair mussed from the hat he had just pulled off. He was already in the middle of a sentence when his voice came through, apologizing for being so late, and it took him a moment to notice that something was wrong. What is it, he said, what happened? I couldn't bring myself to speak for a minute and then I spoke like a child, I said I have to tell you something, I'm sorry, please don't get mad. What is it, he said again, a little frightened now, just tell me. And I did, watching his face as I told him about Mitko's visit and the clinic and what they had said. I didn't know how he would respond; I thought he would be angry, I was even afraid he might end everything between us. But he only took a somewhat deeper breath and said All right, I'll get tested, it's not a big deal, right, the worst case is a shot. Calm down, he said, and I was flooded with gratitude and relief. I was surprised he took it so calmly, more calmly than I had; I was usually the more dependable one, older and more settled, and after we logged off Skype I wondered if his calm would last, or whether he was just shocked at what I had told him, experiencing a kind of blankness before worry set in. And I was right, the next morning I woke to find my in-box full of e-mails he had sent through the night, each more anxious than the last. He had just graduated university and was still without a job, entirely dependent on his parents; he would have to ask them for money, he wrote, which would mean telling them the whole story. He had only recently told them about me, in the process coming out to them; how could he tell them he might have syphilis, he asked me, what would they think. He was frantic by the last e-mail he sent, and I felt horrible for what I had done. We spoke again when he woke, and I told him that I would wire him money, of course I would pay for everything, I

said, after all it was all my fault. Though I braced myself for
his anxiety to turn to resentment and then to blame, it never
did. By Sunday night he had regained his resolve: we would
go to our respective clinics in the morning, we agreed, we
would be treated, it would all be over soon.

I had put the computer away and settled into bed to read
when the buzzer rang. I knew who it was, of course, but I
still stepped out onto the balcony to look. Mitko stood
below, bareheaded against the cold, peering up to catch sight
of me. He smiled when he saw me, and I held my hand out
to him in a staying motion, as if patting something down,
before going back in to quickly put on the clothes I had left
crumpled on the floor. We had agreed, R. and I, that when
Mitko returned I shouldn't let him into my apartment, that
we should speak outside or go somewhere else; I don't like
the idea of him there, R. said, and really he thought I should
cut him off entirely. Why would you see him again, he had
asked me several times over the last days, you don't owe
him anything, you've already helped him, and if you keep
helping him there will be no end to it, he'll take and keep
on taking. You know he doesn't care about you, R. said in
one of our conversations, you were never friends or anything
else. I did know this, and so I found it difficult to explain the
obligation I felt, the sense that I couldn't, whatever else might
happen, simply cut Mitko adrift, though I had tried to do
that before, and maybe I would have to do it again. You
want to be the big American, R. said in a final charge, you
think you can fix things, you want to save him. And maybe
that was part of it; certainly there was a tenderness in
me that Mitko struck as no one else did, and I hated that,
for all his sometimes brutality, he was finally so helpless in a
world that took little heed of him. I did want to help him,
but I no longer believed, if I ever had, that Mitko could be
drawn in any permanent way out of what had become his

life. I knew I couldn't save him, but how could I explain to R., especially to him, the feeling of inevitability I had whenever Mitko appeared, as though we were in a story that had already been written.

He was waiting patiently when I stepped outside into the cold, standing beside the door and drawing on a cigarette that he left in his mouth as he held his hand out in greeting. *K'vo ima*, he asked, glancing up at the dark apartment, what's wrong? A friend is staying with me, I said, the lie R. had told me to use, and Mitko nodded, *Yasno*, I get it. Your friend from Portugal, he said, the obvious assumption, though I was taken aback to hear any mention from him of R., and I quickly shook my head, as if dismissing the thought of him from the air. No, I said, just a friend, and then, before he could ask anything else, Are you hungry, should we go somewhere to eat? We began walking slowly together over the ice, which was thick and many-layered on the sidewalk. Mitko was wearing the same clothes I had last seen him in, the same thin jacket, but he seemed unbothered by the cold, and in general he looked better: he had showered and shaved, his clothes were clean, and looking down, I saw that the canvas sneakers had been replaced by short leather boots, well-worn but sturdy. A friend gave them, Mitko said when I asked, shrugging his shoulders, they're not so nice but they do the job, they're better than the others. We turned to the right just past my building, down a side street that was less traveled and so especially treacherous now, and despite my boots I slipped several times, once nearly falling. Careful, Mitko said, grabbing me and holding me steady, surer-footed than I, and once I had regained my balance he squeezed me hard around the shoulders, leaving his arm there as we continued picking our way to the main boule-vard. There was a McDonald's on this street open twenty-four hours; it was always well lit and there were always people there, as R. had reminded me; it would be a good place if I had to meet with Mitko, he said, a safe place.

I expected Mitko to load his tray with far more than he could eat, as he usually did when I bought him food, but he only ordered a sandwich, fries, and at my insistence a milkshake, which he had never had before, he said, it had never occurred to him to try one. Mitko grabbed the milkshake as soon as the server set it down and put the straw to his lips, and it was a joy to see his eyes widen with pleasure when he tasted it. We walked with his tray to the most secluded corner, as far as we could get from the other diners, a few couples, one large group of friends. To the right of our table there was a closed glass door leading to a room for children's parties. The room was dark now, and the door was locked, as Mitko found when he tried to turn the knob; but we could make out bits of the brightly colored interior, the plastic cubes for climbing, plush seats in the shapes of cartoon characters. It disquieted me somehow; it was a whole world molded for a kind of carelessness I doubted had anything to do with childhood, a carelessness I couldn't remember ever feeling. Mitko sat and tore into his food, not pausing until almost all of it was gone. Then he looked up, almost embarrassed, as if for a moment he had forgotten I was there. *Kak si*, he said, smiling a little, and I said I was fine, a little tired maybe, but all right. It's late, he said apologetically, I know you go to sleep early, I wouldn't have rung the bell except I saw your light. This was untrue, of course, as we both knew, and maybe I spoke a little brusquely when I said Why did you come to see me, do you need something, but he brushed this aside, asking me instead if I had been to the clinic yet, if I had been tested. Yes, I said, I have to go again for a second test tomorrow, but the first was positive, I know I have it. Mitko looked at me silently, and then Oh, he said, I'm sorry, and it sounded genuine, more so as he said it again, *suzhalyavam*, I'm sorry. But I dismissed this, waving my hand a little in the air. I have it from you, I said, probably my friend has it from me, and you got it from someone, too; it's an infection, I said, there's no guilt, you don't need to be sorry. Mitko looked surprised at this, that I had passed up an advantage, but he nodded in acknowledgment nonetheless. And you, I said, are you better, have the pills helped, but he jerked his head, the single vertical motion that means no here, like a door slamming shut. No, they haven't helped, and gesturing to his crotch, I still have the same problem, he said, using the word he had used before, as if for a leaking faucet. I went to the clinic again, he said, I have to get the injections, the pills aren't strong enough. It's dangerous for me, he went on, the medicine is very strong, and I already have problems with my liver, I told you that. I nodded, remembering what he had said about his weeks in the hospital in Varna, which he had spoken of with more horror than of prison. So it's dangerous, he went on, but I have to do it, to get rid of this other thing. *Suzhalyavam*, I said, repeating his word, I'm sorry. And it's expensive, he went on, looking up at me to make the most of my sympathy, the shots cost much more than the pills, one hundred leva, he said, and then quickly added, but that's for all three shots, after that I'm done. He hadn't asked me for anything, but of course the request was there, it seemed cruel to make him say it. *Dobre*, I said, okay, so I'll help you, you don't need to worry. Some tension I hadn't quite registered in him released as he smiled, and I realized that he had been worried, unsure whether my feeling for him would stretch so far. Thank you, he said, and then, you are a true friend, *istinski priyatel*, and I was disconcerted by the pleasure I took in his saying it.

Mitko turned his attention back to the food on his tray, what was left of it, determined not to let anything go to waste. Wanting to get away from him for a moment, I pushed my chair back and stood, saying I would be right back. The bathroom was near the table we had chosen, just across from the locked playroom that seemed to me so oddly baleful. It was small, with a single stall and urinal and a sink mounted against the wall. I stepped up to the urinal, fishing myself out for form's sake but feeling no urgency to piss; I closed my eyes instead and breathed deeply, grateful to be free from Mitko and what he had made me feel, that pleasure that was too sharp. I would wonder, later, whether that feeling itself was an invitation for what happened next, whether I allowed Mitko to see it; but I don't think so, I think I was surprised when I heard or felt the door open, felt more than heard, I think, the tiny shift in pressure, the resistance of the air collapsing like my own resistance, which was swept aside when I felt the sudden warmth of Mitko behind me. I had known it was he when the door opened, it never occurred to me it could be anyone else, as it never occurred to me to tell him to stop, or occurred with so little force it was lost in the sweep of my excitement. There wasn't a lock on the door, we could have been interrupted, and maybe the risk heightened my pleasure as Mitko pressed his whole length against me, placing his feet beside mine and leaning his torso into my spine, his breath hot on my neck. This was reality, I felt with a strange relief, this was where I belonged, and I thought of R., though it shames me to recall it, as though our life together, open and sunlit and lasting, were entirely without substance; I felt it disappear, simply disappear, like a flammable shadow, and part of me was glad to feel it go. Mitko's mouth pressed at my neck and his hands reached beneath my shirt, touching me as he knew I liked to be touched, remembering exactly though so much time had passed. He pressed into me harder, forcing me forward, and I braced myself with one hand against the tile while I felt him grind against me; he wanted me to know that he was hard, that he wanted it too, that he was ready to do again what we had done so often. With my other hand I jerked myself off, I had gotten hard at his first touch, at the first intimation of that touch, and I was swept forward in a single motion, quick and reckless, swept forward by Mitko, the weight of him against me and his hands, and then suddenly his teeth at my neck, until I came with a pleasure I hadn't known in months, that maybe I had never known with R. For a moment, as I let my head fall until my forehead lay next to my arm, before I could feel anything else I was grateful to Mitko. He stayed with me a little longer, wrapping his arms around me more tightly, as if he were holding me in place; and then there was a last pressure of his lips on my neck and he was gone.

I left my head resting on the tile, taking deep breaths, feeling my organism settle with a sensation like the clicking of metal as it cools. Without opening my eyes, I pulled on the lever to flush the urinal, then again, and then a third time. I was used to feeling regret in such moments, of course, sometimes I thought it was part of my pleasure, like a bitter taste making a flavor more rich; but I felt something stronger now, I was sick, I was infectious, and children came here, I thought, remembering that locked room as I flushed the urinal again and again. Then I stepped into the stall and unwound a mass of toilet paper, which I wet at the sink and used to wipe down the lever I had just touched, as well as the wall where I had braced myself, though there could be no danger there; and then I began wiping down the porcelain itself, inside and out. I knew the whole performance was excessive, I was wiping surfaces unlikely ever to be touched, but I kept at it as the paper dissolved in my hand. Finally I carried the wet mass to the toilet, and then I stood for some time at the sink, washing my hands. Only then did I let myself think of R., as I looked at myself in the mirror, my face still flushed. He loves you, I said, whispering the words out loud. And then I said it again.

I saw that Mitko had cleared the table when I stepped out of the bathroom. Only the paper cup of the milkshake was left, and he leaned over it with his elbows planted on the table, looking at me with his head quizzically cocked. He looked like a child, I thought, as I had so often before. He watched me with a kind of guarded expectancy, as if he knew he hadn't acted strictly as he should, but thought he had been so charming he could still expect a reward. When he asked me if everything was all right, I said Yes yes, everything was fine. *Malko sme ludichki*, he said then, his face breaking into its smile, a real smile, full voltage: we're a little crazy; and I had to agree that this was so, smiling at him weakly in response. But my smile faded quickly, and without sitting down I said that we should go. Yes, Mitko replied, your friend is waiting, and before I remembered my earlier excuse I thought of R. He stood up, then took his cup and sucked loudly at the straw one last time, gathering all the sweetness he could. The cold was brutal after the warmth of the restaurant, but I paused to give Mitko the money he had asked for, taking the five new bills from my wallet and folding them once as I passed them to him. Thank you, he said, closing the money in his fist and bringing it to his heart, thank you a lot, *naistina*, I mean it. It's nothing, I said, you need it; and then quickly I asked him how he wanted to get home, whether by metro or by bus. But it was late now, and a Sunday, and neither of us was sure how late the metro would run. There was a bus stop across the boulevard that would get him downtown, and we made our way there together, the slush of the day's traffic already frozen in the quiet street. Mitko walked confidently in his new shoes, a few steps ahead of me, no longer quite so attentive, I couldn't help thinking, now that he had what he had come for; and he looked around restlessly, as if he were frustrated by the empty street. There was only one other person waiting at the flimsy structure of plastic and corrugated tin, a thirty-something man in a heavy coat, huddling away from the wind and curled around the cigarette in his hand. He glanced at us and then quickly looked away, but Mitko spoke to him without hesitation, calling him *bratle*, brother, asking first for a cigarette and then, when this was handed over, for a light. *Dobre*, I said after this transaction, all right, I'll leave you here, I should get back, and Mitko stuck the cigarette in his mouth, holding his hand out to me for a brief farewell. Then he stepped out from under the shelter, and, though it meant exposing himself to the wind, turned his face in the direction from which the bus would come.

The buses of the 76 line are old and in poor repair, and the one that finally pulled up the next morning looked like all the others, square and painted a flat metallic green. It was double length, the two compartments joined by a great hinge in the center, the seam sealed with accordioned plastic that gave and took up slack as the two halves struggled against each other on the poor roads. The plastic was torn in places, letting in drafts that were painfully cold and yet did nothing somehow to relieve the stifling heat. My stop was early enough on the route that I was able to find a seat, and I wiped the window with my sleeve, clearing a half circle in the condensation, though it fogged over again almost at once. At each stop more people got on and only a few got off; by Tsarigradsko Shose, the boulevard leading downtown, the bus was full, and a large older woman had taken the seat next to me. In the more restricted space I gave up trying to keep the window clear, letting it steam over entirely, and shifted my attention to the inside of the bus. The aisles were filling up, and so was the open space around the contraptions for punching tickets, just a row or two from my seat, and the larger space farther up where the two halves of the bus were joined, a circular panel in the floor covering the hinge or joint between them. It was a difficult place to ride; older people avoided it, though there was a railing to help manage the rocking motion that could sometimes, depending on the driver's mood, be quite violent. I remembered one afternoon that fall, just after school and so before the evening rush, when I watched a group of male students take turns standing there, riding without holding on to the railing, bending their knees and throwing out their arms in a surfer's pose, laughing as they were thrown off balance. No one was in the mood for that now, there was a Monday morning dourness in the way the men gripped the rail. The bus grew hotter as even more people got on, and the air took on a winter smell I had grown accustomed to, of wet wool and cigarettes and even this early of beer.

I had begun to sweat, and I glanced at the latch at the top of the window, wishing I could reach up and pull it down. But I didn't dare; everyone would have been upset, people here are convinced they can catch their death from a draft. There was a man standing in the space just in front of me, leaning against the window, who was moving slightly, not just with the bus but with a motion of his own, shifting his weight forward and then back, his coat dragging against the window. It was while he was leaning forward that I saw a fly on the pane of glass behind him. It was still, maybe numbed by the cold of the window, a common housefly that must have ridden in from the heated interior of someone's apartment via the heated interior of someone's clothes. In the summer flies are common on buses, of course, a buzzing nuisance, but this one seemed special; it must have survived against all odds to make it here, so deep in the season. It clung to the pane despite the shuddering of the bus, until finally it made a tiny movement upward, like an exploratory step up the glass. When the man leaned back, his coat falling over it again, I almost cried out to stop him. I waited for the fly to reappear, unable to look away from the spot I had last seen it. I had forgotten the stifling heat and the general misery of the ride in my concern for the creature and in my relief, when the man shifted again, to find it still intact. For the next few minutes I watched as the man leaned forward and back and the fly was covered and revealed. Almost every time the coat was lifted it made another movement upward toward the point where the man's shoulder met the glass; Don't do that, I said under my breath, that's the wrong way. It was ridiculous to care so much, I knew, it was just a fly, why should it matter; but it did matter, at least while I watched it. That's all care is, I thought, it's just looking at a thing long enough, why should it be a question of scale? This seemed like a hopeful thought at first, but then it's hard to look at things, or to look at them truly, and we can't look at many at once, and it's so easy to look away.

Downtown, at Orlov Most, Eagle Bridge, the bus finally got less crowded, with half or so of the passengers stepping off and many fewer getting on. The woman beside me stood up, much to my relief, and the man leaning against the glass left too, moving with the others to escape the bus. I looked eagerly for the housefly, and when I saw no sign of it I stood, before the new riders climbed on, and scanned the floor to see if it had fallen. But there was nothing there either, and I sat down again at a loss. There were only a few more stops before we entered Gotse Delchev and turned onto residential streets, and since I was unfamiliar with the route now I moved to be near the door, where I leaned out to read the name of each station that we passed. But I needn't have worried; the polyclinic had its own stop and several people got off there, leaving the bus almost empty as we stepped down into the snow. It was a broad gray concrete structure of four or five stories, much larger than the clinic near the school, nearly a hospital. The steps leading up to the entrance were perilous, packed with ice, as was the unusable wheelchair ramp to my left. I climbed up carefully, planting both feet on a single stair before chancing another, feeling how easily I could lose my footing, feeling elderly, and wondering how the genuinely infirm could possibly manage. The ground floor of the building was a large, echoing space that seemed unfinished; the floors were untreated, little more than concrete, the walls coated in bare plaster. There was no reception or information desk, only a large notice board with the departments organized by floor, the doctors' names on long plastic strips that could be taken out and replaced. I had the page with the name of the department I needed, but the woman from the clinic had written in a quick cursive hand I couldn't quite make out. Some of the words on the board were familiar, ophthalmology, gynecology, but the transliterations were awkward, I had to sound them all out, and there were several I couldn't make any sense of at all. As I looked around in confusion, I saw a woman in a white coat coming down the large central stairs, holding a plastic cup of coffee and clearly on her way out for a break, though the day had hardly begun. Excuse me, I said, using the politest form, *proshtavaite*, forgive me, as I held my page out to her, can you help me find this? She took it from me, and then her eyes flicked up once, from the paper to my face, almost without expression. She pointed me toward a far corner, where there was a sign that read *Dermatologiya i Venerologiya*. I recognized the first word, but the second took me a moment; we say venereal disease in English, of course, but I had never heard of a venereology department, and I wondered whether the word was used in the States. By its Latin roots it should have meant the study of love, and I wondered too how often that made it the right word for the people who came here, and whether it was the right word for my own predicament.

I pulled open the door and stepped into a long bare hall-way of offices, lined at intervals with benches bolted to the walls. It was almost empty, I saw with relief; an elderly couple occupied one bench, a teenage boy another. At the far end there was a door that led outside, and above the last office on the left I saw a sign for registration. The door to the of-fice was closed, but at my knock a voice called for me to come in. A middle-aged woman was sitting at a desk with a newspaper spread in front of her, her right hand resting by a cup of coffee, clearly absorbed in a morning routine. She didn't look up as I entered, her eyes still scanning the page, and turned to me only as I spoke, with an interest sparked, I suspected, by my accent. She returned my greeting and then looked at me expectantly, waiting for me to explain why I was there. I've received a positive result on a test, I said, handing her the note I had been given by the other clinic, I'm here for a second one to confirm it. All right, she said, rising slowly from the desk, as if loath to leave her cof-fee; have you had any symptoms, she asked, any sores, using the word *rani*, wounds, and when I said that I hadn't, or none I had noticed, I knew they could be painless and small, she asked why I had gotten tested in the first place, whether I had any reason to think I might be infected. I hadn't antic-ipated the question, and I paused before responding. A friend came to see me, I said finally, he told me that he had this sickness, he said that I should be tested. She raised her eye-brows just slightly at this, and then she said So you had contact with this person, using that word, which is the same in the two languages, *kontakt*; and I repeated it back to her, looking her directly in the eyes, Yes, I had contact with him. I wouldn't accept the shame she seemed to want me to feel, and she acknowledged this, I thought, dropping her gaze as she reached past me to open the door. *Dobre*, she said, all right, follow me. She made quick work of me in a room across the hall, not speaking as she swabbed and drew blood, and once again I was surprised by the lack of gloves. Then she ushered me out with the promise that someone would see me when I returned that afternoon for my results.

I couldn't bear the thought of spending hours in that long hallway with its bare benches, still occupied by the same patients, or would-be patients, who hadn't moved and seemed resigned to a long wait. I needed to walk, even if it was hard going in the snow, so I exited through the door next to the registration office and descended a long ramp leading to the street. The air had warmed, it looked to be a beautiful day, sunny and clear as few had been that season, and already the snow and ice had softened, the surface giving way just slightly, slick and wet. I thought of Mitko and his new shoes, the old ones would already have been soaked through. I was dry in my winter boots, though they didn't help much with the ice, and I made my way slowly down the ramp and then across the little street that ran the length of the building toward the main boulevard. It was a pleasant neighborhood, Gotse Delchev, prosperous and older than Mladost, with more trees and green spaces; it might even be lovely come spring, I thought. There were still the apartment blocks, that Soviet model of collective life, but there wasn't the same randomness and glut here as in Mladost, where in the chaos after the fall of the old system space was snatched up and structures built, or half-built, without rhyme or reason, cheap and unplanned. Here, in Gotse Delchev, there were fewer new buildings, and the original plan of the neighborhood was still visible, its geometrical shapes. The shops I passed weren't just the single-shelf affairs of Mladost, the little markets made up of prefabricated shacks; they were urban, even elegant, or at least aiming toward an idea of elegance. In front of some of them paths had been shoveled through the snow, something almost unheard of here. Even in the cold, and even at an hour when many people were at work, I passed people shopping or walking their dogs, and young people, university students maybe, busy about their lives, so that the streets I walked seemed vibrant to me, more vibrant than my own. But then almost everywhere I went I imagined a place more accommodating of the life I wanted, as if happiness were a matter of streets or parks, as maybe to a point it is; and with R. away for so long I was accustomed to thinking of my real life existing in some distant place or future time, projecting forward in a way that I was afraid might keep me from living fully where I was. R. must be up by now, I thought, he must be heading for his own clinic, with whatever feelings of apprehension or shame, with whatever feelings of remorse.

I turned onto the large and busy boulevard that marked the neighborhood's edge, though this meant facing into the wind, which charged down it unimpeded by buildings or trees. Several blocks ahead I could see something that looked like a construction site, though not of the kind scattered throughout Sofia, for malls or apartments; there was a single concrete pillar rising above the billboards that lined the streets, I couldn't imagine at first what it was for. When I reached it, I saw that the billboards, which were faded and worn at the edges, displayed information about the construction of a cathedral, and that the date set for its completion had passed by several years. There was a sketch of what the cathedral would look like on one of the boards, along with its name, SVETI PURVOMUCHENIK STEFAN, Saint Stefan the First Martyr, I thought, puzzling out the roots for first and pain, the suffix that makes a word signify a person. Printed in a larger font than the saint's name was the project's corporate sponsor, one of the country's biggest banks. The site was surrounded by a fence draped with green mesh, which was torn away in places. No one was building anything now, and it didn't look like anyone had been working there for a long time. The pillar was the only section they had really begun, though maybe they had laid foundations for the rest, I couldn't tell because of the snow. There was also an arch, I could see now; it peeled off from the side of the pillar, and next to it were a few steps leading up to a small platform. It was going to be the entrance, then, and the pillar must have been intended for the bell tower, though they hadn't gotten very far; there were thin metal rods extending naked a few feet beyond the concrete, an aspiration, so far as I could tell, entirely abandoned.

I made my way across the road, two lanes on one side of the concrete median and two on the other, the ice more perilous than the traffic. The fence wasn't really meant to keep anyone out, or not anymore; the metal posts were planted in concrete blocks one could move easily enough, as someone had already done where the segment of chain link was unsecured, creating a passageway I slipped through. The arch was graceful, despite the cheap material it was made of, and the whole site was like a ruin, or a ruin in reverse, caught rising rather than falling. The ground was strewn with beer bottles, cheap plastic jugs sticking up through the snow; there was no telling how long they had been there. I climbed the few stairs to the platform, which was sheltered from the snow by the arch, and here there was more refuse, a profusion of cigarette butts and plastic bags and, here and there, the discarded wrapper of a condom, the top strip torn and bent, opened hurriedly, I imagined, gripped by fingers or teeth. It hadn't been entirely abandoned, then, and I thought of the teenagers who must use it to escape apartments that often enough house three generations. I looked up at the arch, and something in me responded to the familiar shape of it, though I haven't been to a church in years, or not as anything but a tourist. I thought of R., wondering if he had gotten tested yet, if he was waiting for the result; I hated that I wasn't with him, that there was no one he could ask to go in my place, that he was there because of me. I worried it would make him regret having met me at all; I wondered if I thought it should. Maybe they were a mistake, my years in this country, maybe the illness I had caught was just a confirmation of it. What had I done but extend my rootlessness, the series of false starts that became more difficult to defend as I got older? I think I hoped I would feel new in a new country, but I wasn't new here, and if there was comfort in the idea that my habitual unease had a cause, that if I was ill-fitted to the place there was good reason, it was a false comfort, a way of running away from real remedy. But then I didn't truly believe there was a remedy, I thought as I stepped down from the platform into the snow, walking back to the boulevard, and how could I regret the choices that had brought me, by whatever path, to R., any more than I could regret those that had led to Mitko and to moments that flared in my memory, that I knew I would cherish whatever their consequences.

I found a café, where I took refuge for a few hours with a book and bad coffee. When I returned to the polyclinic I was greeted by a different woman, who was much warmer than the first, even friendly as she told me that the test results were ready and that the doctor was available; she knocked on the office door and peered in briefly to announce my presence, and then told me to take a seat on the bench beside it. Just a minute, she said, she'll call you in, though I waited much longer than that. The hallway was empty now, there were just two cleaning women standing at the other end, chatting beside a cart and mop, oblivious to who I was or why I was there. Soon it would all be over, I thought, remembering what R. had said; I would speak to the doctor and get my shot, and then I would be back in that cleaner life he and I had made together. It was only at the second or third shout from inside the room that I realized a voice, already exasperated, was calling for me to enter. I stood quickly, disconcerted, the more so as I opened the door to find a woman glaring fiercely at me from behind a desk. She stood as I walked in, but didn't greet me or extend her hand, merely nodding at my murmured *Dobur den*. She was a slight woman, not quite young, and I was taken aback by her appearance, which suggested an idea of beauty at once ubiquitous and mocked here, a hypersexualized style associated with a certain kind of fashionable wealth. She was elaborately made up, with heavy eye shadow and glossy lips, and her hair was teased and styled into an enormous, unmoving mass. Her medical coat was pulled tight, and beneath it she wore a skirt of some vaguely reflective material and extremely high heels. She spoke Bulgarian in an odd way, very quickly and somehow at once clipped and indistinct, as though the words were a crisp fruit she bit into to find that it was soft. We have the results of the second test, she said, there's no doubt now that you have this illness, which is something very serious for you, serious and dangerous, for you and for anyone with whom you have sexual contact of any kind. There was an odd formality to her speech, as though she were reciting a government text, as perhaps she was, and she asked me questions I had already been asked, whether I had had any wounds or sores on my genitals, but not only there, also in my mouth, beneath my tongue. Nothing I've noticed, I said, nothing unusual, though I had had sores in my mouth, they aren't uncommon for me, they've come and gone since I was a child. This gave me pause, and the woman cocked her head just slightly. Are you sure, she said, a note of suspicion clear in her tone. I had heard university friends, medical students, complain that patients always lie, which they said with the same professional knowingness and exaspera-

tion I saw in the look the doctor gave me now, and if it was
true in general it must be especially true here, in this room
where there was such humiliation in revelation, where guarding a secret felt so much like guarding the self. Yes, I said, I'm
certain.

She seemed to sigh at this, in acknowledgment or frustration, I'm not sure which, and then she said something I
didn't catch at all, a quick and sharp command. I hesitated a
moment; sometimes there's a kind of delay in processing the
words and it's as though I hear them again, or see them almost, laid out end to end as if on a page. But nothing came
now, not a single word, and before I could ask she repeated
herself more loudly, as one sometimes does when speaking
to foreigners, as though it helps. I'm sorry, I said, feeling like
a child, I don't understand. The doctor closed her eyes, just
slightly longer than a blink, and then she took what I thought
must have been a steadying breath before saying something I did understand, Lower your pants, though I hesitated again, bringing my hand to my belt buckle but not
yet undoing the clasp. This was too much for her, apparently,
my failure to comply, and unable to contain her annoyance,
she said Go on, I need to see your dick, using a word that
while not quite vulgar wasn't clinical either. It shocked me a
little, though it wasn't just the word that was a breach in
decorum, it was also the pronoun she used, the informal *ti*.
I had never really felt the force of this before; knowing how
to address someone was always hard for me, we don't have
those nuances in English verbs, or not anymore. But I felt
the difference it made now, it was like a change of temperature, and it eroded further the dignity I wanted to preserve.
I lost that dignity entirely as I exposed myself, and then
lifted my penis for her to inspect, pulling it to the right and
the left as she directed, exposing all surfaces to her view.
Finally she was satisfied, motioning for me to cover myself,

and turned away to a little table beside her desk, where there was a blunt metal container and a large wad of cotton. She tore off some of this and dipped it quickly in the canister before handing me the sodden mass, the smell of it antiseptic and foul. For your hands, she said, and then turned again dismissively toward her desk.

Taka, she said then, once she was seated, while I was still fumbling with my clothes, so, the best treatment for this disease is an injection of penicillin, but as unfortunately now there is no penicillin available, this course of treatment is not possible. Wait, I said, interrupting her, and maybe intending to reclaim something, to mount some challenge, how is that possible, not to have such a basic thing? But she was unperturbed, holding up a single hand to silence me. The manufacturer of this drug is in Austria, she said, and they have stopped distributing it to us; for four months it has been impossible to find in Bulgaria. Anywhere, I asked, not quite believing it, and said again, how is it possible, but she shrugged her shoulders and went on. You can check this for yourself if you like, of course, but I can tell you that no one in Bulgaria has had this drug for months, and no one can tell you when we will have it again. It is available in Greece, I think, she said, I will write you a prescription if you'd like to go there for your treatment. How could I go there, I said, I have a job here, I can't go to Greece. *Kakto i da e*, she said, however that may be, and then went on to propose an alternative. The second best treatment is a course of pills, she said; it is not the best option, but most of the time it does the job. She reached for a pad at the edge of her desk. You will take the pills for two weeks, she said, and then after three months you will be tested again, to see whether the treatment has been successful. I had read all I could find about treatment on the Internet, and I knew that a two-week course of pills wasn't always enough, especially if it was an old infection, in which case four weeks was more likely to work. If there's doubt, I ventured, shouldn't I take the pills for a longer time, but she held up her hand before I had finished speaking, and began reciting a text that this time I was sure was an official script. In making these recommendations, she said, I'm following the guidelines of the Ministry of Health and Prevention, *zdraveopazvaneto*, I'm not sure of the best translation; should you wish to follow another treatment, I cannot accept responsibility for the consequences. I was *Vie* again, she had returned to the formal address, and I felt like this was a further humiliation, though I couldn't say why. And if I accept the responsibility for those consequences, I said, as she began writing on her pad, will you write me a prescription for four weeks? She continued writing, and in the same tone of officious formality began to say again that she could only follow the Ministry's regulations, but then she paused and looked up. In general, she said, there is not a problem in using a prescription twice. This was true, I would find; the prescription wasn't dated, and later that afternoon, when the pharmacist handed it back to me along with my pills, there wasn't any sign on it that it had already been filled, I could use it as many times as I wanted. She finished writing and held the paper out for me to take, remaining in her seat so that I had to step forward and reach over the large desk. And that's all, she said, releasing me, you will return in three months for another test.

I turned toward the door, desperate to leave, exhausted by my encounter with this woman, who had been *uzhasna*, I thought, awful, thinking it half in Bulgarian and half in my own language, which I returned to as if stepping onto more solid ground. One more thing, I heard the woman say behind me, drawing me back, her chair squeaking as she stood. I turned to see her moving toward another side table, where there was a large ledger book lying open. It was like the book in which we kept track of our classes each day at my school, signing for every hour we taught. Because of its danger, the woman said, the Ministry requires that we report all cases of this illness. I felt a sudden concern, wondering if this would complicate my stay in the country, my visa that must be renewed each year; but I thought also it would be a way not to choose, if I was forced to leave, it would almost be a relief. Then I looked down at the page, where in a quick, not quite cursive Cyrillic I saw that she had gotten my name wrong, putting down my first and middle names but leaving off the last; there wouldn't be any consequence, I thought, they wouldn't be able to find me at all. In the large box next to this mistaken name they had glued in a strip of paper with a typed statement, a pledge of sorts not to donate blood until tests showed I was no longer a danger. The woman laid her finger, with its long painted nail, on the blank line beneath this, saying I had to sign it before I left. I did so, putting my initials down with a little flourish, entirely illegible. She closed the book as soon as I was finished, using both hands to hold the long pages in their place as she folded it shut. I can go now, I said, phrasing it half as a question, and she nodded, though as I laid my hand on the doorknob I heard her voice again. Tell me, she said, did you have this disease when you came here, did you bring it with you? I paused, keeping my hand on the door, and then without turning I replied Of course not, it's something I picked up here. And then, as I opened the door, with a bitterness I didn't plan, A souvenir of your beautiful country, I said.

I closed the door behind me and sat down again on the bench. I was eager to leave but I hadn't paid yet, and before I could speak to anyone I needed a moment to myself. So I sat, staring at nothing, at the floor, determined not to see anything for a while; I sat with my head in my hands, and then with my hands over my eyes, the heel of each palm fitted to the socket. It was a posture of distress, I suppose, though it wasn't quite distress that I felt. I didn't understand the bitterness with which I had spoken, bitterness not just toward the woman but toward the place, this country I had chosen; I hadn't known I felt it, and I wondered how deep it went. There was something else troubling me, too, and after I had sat for a little while I realized that what the doctor had told me contradicted Mitko's story. The last time I had seen him he said he needed money for injections, that the pills hadn't worked, but it must have been a lie; there weren't any injections to be had, pills were the only treatment he could get. For a moment it was as if I hung suspended, unsure of what I felt. I didn't know why I was so surprised, I knew Mitko couldn't be trusted, that he would do or say almost anything for money; and this was something I could hardly resent, when it had given me access to him in the first place. But I was angry, I felt I had been made a fool. Maybe I imagined we had gotten past this somehow, that the sickness we shared established a kind of solidarity between us, a shared ground. And I had been generous, too, I had helped him without getting anything in return. But that wasn't true, I thought suddenly, I had gotten something in return, he had made sure of that when he followed me into the bathroom and made me see how much I wanted him. He hadn't allowed me to be generous, that had been the point of what he had done. I had wanted to give without taking, but it must have been humiliating for him, not to have anything to bargain with, and I wondered now if I had liked his humiliation, if that was the pleasure I took in my generosity, that I was humiliating him in giving him what he needed while claiming not to need anything back. R. had been right, there would be no end to it, not just to Mitko's taking but to my own false motives; there could never be any shared ground between us, we would never find a way to be decent to each other. I had to end it, I knew, I had to give up the pleasure of him, not just the obvious pleasure but the pleasure of being kind, of what I had taken for kindness and now feared was something else.

I heard someone walking toward me and took my palms from my eyes, which were dazzled by the sudden light. It was the woman from the office, standing by the bench and looking at me with concern, and I was embarrassed, realizing I had made a quiet spectacle of myself. *Vsichko nared li e*, she asked, is everything all right, is everything in order, rather, *red* being the word for line or sequence; is everything in its place is what it really means, and I thought to myself when was it ever. But of course I said yes, that short syllable, saying it twice in quick succession, *da da*, as if to say what a question, how could it be otherwise, and she nodded at this as though she believed it, and then took a seat beside me on the bench. I was surprised by the sudden closeness, flinching a little as if she might mean me harm. She wasn't a young woman, but there was a sense of vitality about her that made me think of the Bulgarian phrase *zryala vuzrast*, ripe age, which they use for the period before one is truly old. She was large, but she carried her weight like a sign of health, her frame softened by well-being. It occurred to me that she was the first person I had seen in these institutions who didn't seem exhausted or exasperated; it's a talent some people have, being at ease, or seem to have, I know such impressions can be wrong. *Ne se pritesnyavai*, this woman said, don't worry, *ne e fatalno*, it's not so serious, you'll do the treatment and get better, soon it will be behind you. She was being kind, simply kind, and I looked at her for a moment before I said thank you, and then, because it was inadequate to what I felt, I said it again. And your friend, she went on, and I noted that she too was addressing me informally; before I had been *Vie* and *gospodinut*, the gentleman, but now I was set on a new footing. And this was part of her kindness, so that I felt the other side of that nuance my language doesn't have, that if it is a loss of dignity it can be a gain of warmth, something that seemed to me now very dear. Your friend, how is he, she asked, has he been to see someone, is he getting treatment? He is, I said, though I realized I wasn't sure if that was true, I didn't know where the money I had given him had gone. She nodded, It's important that he does, she said, make sure he finishes it, otherwise he won't get better. All right, I said, I will, and she braced her palms against her thighs and stood. Come on, then, she said, let's go to the office so you can pay and get home.

I was warmed by her kindness as I made my way back to Mladost, the bus nearly empty, the evening rush still hours away. I thought of Mitko on the long ride, feeling sure my decision was the right one, and feeling too that it would be difficult to keep. When I talked to R. that evening, he told me that he had been tested in the morning and received his shot in the afternoon; and I was glad that it seemed to be something he had put behind him as he dressed to go out for dinner with friends. I was feeling better, too. I had eaten already and was sitting and reading in the main room, relaxing for a bit before bed; it had been a long day, I would go to sleep early. I didn't have any desire to see Mitko, and when I heard the quick bleat of the buzzer I was tempted to ignore it. But he could see my light from the street, he knew I was home, and anyway it would be better to get it over with now, I thought, while I was still sure of what I had to say. I didn't press the button to release the door or speak to him, but I did turn on the hall lights, which would be acknowledgment enough. I took my time putting on my boots and coat, wrapping a scarf around my neck; it had gotten colder again once the sun went down, but I felt I was wrapping myself up against something else, too, some inner weather against which I had to guard.

Mitko was waiting for me below, his hands jammed into his pockets, his shoulders hunched against the cold. Maybe it was the cold that made him less friendly; he didn't shake my hand or smile, he hardly greeted me at all. I thought you weren't coming, he said sullenly, without any of his usual charm, what took you so long. I have friends over, I said, we're eating dinner, feeling in some way that lying confirmed my resolve, that it was proof of a falseness between us that was irremediable. Mitko shrugged, saying But can we go somewhere else, I don't feel well, it's so cold. No, I said, though it was hard to say it, I'm sorry, I don't have much time, I have to get back to my friends. He made no reply, having expected this, maybe, or maybe the excuse was so evidently false it didn't deserve an answer. I need to go home, he said, I want to be in Varna, I don't have anywhere to sleep here, I don't have any money. He didn't look at me as he said this, looking instead at the ground, or to the side, as if he were ashamed, and as he spoke he shifted his weight back and forth, scuffing the snow with his shoes. Will you help me, he said, still not looking at me, I need forty leva for the bus, that's all, forty leva *samo*, please. He was less sullen than suppliant now, and I hesitated before I answered. Whatever he would actually do with the money I could see he was in need; he was miserable and cold, I was sure he was hungry, and what was it to me, forty leva, now I think I should have given him whatever he wanted. But I didn't give it to him, I said No, Mitko, I'm finished giving you money, *krai*, I said, the end. *Zashto*, he asked, looking up at me sharply, why, repeating it again, *zashto?* I know you didn't get the injections, I said, at the clinic today they said you can't get them in Bulgaria, and I told him that at Tokuda they had said the same, when I called the international hospital to confirm what I had been told. But that's not true, he said, raising his voice in indignation, I got the shot, I'll take you to my clinic, he said, they'll tell you, but I cut him off, saying I didn't want to go anywhere with him. I'm not a liar, Mitko said, standing still now, don't call me a liar, I've never lied to you. I thought I could see him gathering his forces, trying to put on that face I had seen in Varna so many months before; but it was as though he couldn't quite manage it, as though it were beyond him now, and with a sadness I couldn't explain I watched it fade before it had formed. Come on, he said, *are be*, give me the money and I'll go, I won't bother you anymore. But I shook my head. I won't, I said, speaking gently now, I'm through. I touched his shoulder, not sure what I wanted it to mean, and then I turned my back to him and went inside, where I shuddered almost violently at the sudden warmth.

Even with all I fail to understand, living here—the half-caught phrase or gesture, the assumed meaning I can't share—here as nowhere else I have the sense at times of the world tidying itself up for consumption, of a meaning delivered like meat already cut, strangeness of a sudden making sense. Not long ago, for instance, after the end of the whole story with Mitko, I found myself on a train from the coast returning to Sofia. I was dreading the journey as I dread all long trips, with their boredom and confinement, especially in the heat of late summer. And I was all the more apprehensive because I was traveling with my mother, her visit a tentative rapprochement after three years of near estrangement. We hadn't fallen out, exactly, but she was part of that past I had wanted somehow to undo, a past I had felt freer without, and I was uneasy at the thought of her coming here, bringing with her so much of what I had fled. There was the added burden of being a host, heavier since it was my mother's first trip to Europe, her first trip anywhere at all, and she felt a mixture of eagerness and anxiety I had to satisfy and allay. She had scheduled ten days in Bulgaria, most of which we had spent outside of Sofia; I wanted her to see the more beautiful parts of the country, and we were

returning now from Burgas, a seaside city I had long wanted
to visit. We had both been charmed by it, and as we joined
the crowds walking its long piers and rocky beach, there
was a vibrancy in the summer-drunk evenings I had never
felt in Sofia. We hadn't had any of the dramatic scenes I had
anticipated, though we were both fatigued, I thought, by
the care we took to avoid them. But the trip had not been a
failure; I hadn't, as I had feared, been cruel to her, though for
a long time cruelty had been my way of protecting myself
from what I saw as her grasping possessiveness, a desire to
pry that infringed upon my necessary privacy. She had been
careful, after our three years apart, not to impose, and she
maintained a lightness of tone that didn't quite preclude moments of closeness. She spoke of the past in a way she hadn't
before, telling stories of my father, of his early life and of their
life together, for the first time speaking of him without ran-
cor, acknowledging a happiness that was brief and had never
been reclaimed. I was eager for these stories, though I was
cautious, too; I knew that they might draw me back to what
I had left, that they had depths I might be lost in.

When my mother first arrived, I was shocked by how
drawn and worn her face was, how thin and fragile-seeming
her frame. She was unquestionably old now, as she hadn't
been before, and I saw this with a pang as she stepped through
the glass doors at the airport's new terminal, a pang I felt
again as we settled in our seats on the train, arranging our
bags in the unclaimed space between us. I had paid for a
first-class cabin, and on our way to it we passed through six
or seven cars, comfortable and European and aggressively
air-conditioned, to find that our own was the sole unmod-
ernized wagon, a rusted relic of socialism. Its claim to first-
class status lay in the fact that it was divided into four
eight-person cabins, each of which had a glass door that could
be shut, though they all stood open now in the hot unmov-

ing air. I was mortified by this, which I felt as my own failure, though I tried to laugh it off; only in Bulgaria, I said,
and told my mother that now she would have an authentic
Balkan experience. My mother took my lead, dismissing any
discomfort as she arranged her things, even as her discomfort was clear, not least in how she eyed the other passengers
sharing the small space. My mother has always been mis-
trustful of strangers, a part of the timidity or fear that at
times seemed to dominate her life and that I feared I had
inherited, learning from her a hesitancy, a kind of suspicion
or doubt of my forces that had kept me, that might still keep
me, from finding how far they could run. Anything foreign
caused her alarm, as I could see in the way she grasped her
purse, even when she delighted in the newness of what she
had seen. She was uneasy now, too, though any sign of it was
restrained by the politeness that was an imperative almost
equal to her fear. I was relieved to see that our cabin wasn't
full; my mother and I were able to claim an entire side of it
for ourselves, the three other passengers having arranged
themselves to face forward as the train began to move. Of
these three, one was traveling alone, a man in his thirties,
bearded and overweight, a fat paperback open on his lap.
At the opposite end of the bench, by the window, sat an
older woman, very large and wrapped in layers of clothing
despite the heat, and sprawled upon her, half in her lap and
half in the seat beside her, apparently sleeping, there was a
boy of perhaps six or seven. His face was turned toward the
sun, though the woman held one hand above him so that
a shadow fell across his eyes. My mother was immediately
charmed by him, he was the same age as my brother's child,
but my own heart sank at the prospect of the noisy hours
ahead. I wished him a long sleep as I took out my book, I
don't remember now what it was, something in English,
and my mother pulled from her bag the stack of magazines

she carried with her everywhere we went. We settled in to read, my mother and I and the man with his book, which made him laugh out loud every now and again. When the heat got too much for her to bear, my mother would lay her magazine aside or close it and use it as a fan, looking at me with wide eyes and mouthing It's so hot, the peculiar drawn openness of the southern vowel clear even in pantomime. I could only shrug at this, helpless to improve things beyond the opened window and door, which allowed for the occasional draft, though the train moved too slowly and stopped too frequently for anything like a real breeze. I set my book aside often to look out at the landscape as it shifted, at the towns and villages we passed, nearly all of them in disrepair, cottages and little houses falling into themselves. The huge fields were brown and cracked with drought, though they were still worked by huddled figures with bundles on their backs, or by the rare tractor kicking up dust. As we passed these places, it was easy to imagine that we were in a different time, the buildings and natural spaces almost untouched by the modern age, except that so many of the cottages we passed, even the most decrepit, were festooned with the same satellite dishes I knew from my neighborhood in Sofia, some small and modern, others huge and tripodal, discolored with age.

After an hour or so the boy's sleep grew fitful; he turned and kicked his legs, then heaved himself out of the woman's lap and sat blinking as she roused herself in turn. The boy looked around the compartment, at once shyly and openly, his eyes meeting mine briefly before shifting away. Lie back down, I heard the woman say to him, as she put her arm around him to pull him back, but he wasn't tired, he said, and he braced both his arms against her to resist. He was hungry, and the woman rooted around in one of the large bags she had arranged at her feet, pulling out a sandwich wrapped in cellophane, which she folded back before handing it to him. He grabbed it and slid off the bench, standing at the window to watch the landscape as it passed. He was still half-asleep, his eyes glazed over, chewing slowly, mechanically, as if willing himself awake. I was looking at him more than at my book, and at my mother, too, who was watching him and smiling, smiling more broadly whenever he looked her way; but he was shy with her, not quite smiling back. He grew more alert as he ate, taking from his grandmother a bottle of *airan*, yogurt mixed with water, a favorite drink here. He ate more seriously as he woke, taking larger bites and throwing his head back to drink, holding the empty bottle inverted in the air, catching the last drops on his tongue. His grandmother took the trash from him, after which he held his hand in front of her, palm up, and she gave him a small piece of chocolate wrapped in foil. He ate this quickly and without any show of pleasure, and then, when the woman held out her hand for the foil he had crumpled, he made a quick leap and tossed it out the window. She scolded him for this, saying something I couldn't catch, perhaps it was just his name, but he spun around with a broad smile, looking at each of us, as if at once surprised and delighted by his own daring. I tried to look at him sternly, to show an adult solidarity with his grandmother, but my intention gave way before his smile, which was impossibly bright, sure of itself and sure, too, that nothing could resist it for long.

He was a beautiful child, slim and long-limbed, his skin bronzed from his vacation at the sea. He was used to being adored, I thought a little bitterly, despite responding myself to his loveliness. We all felt it; my mother was immediately won over, and even the man across from us smiled over the top of his book. His grandmother pulled him back into his seat, still scolding him, telling him to sleep, they had a long way to go, and then, when he refused, she told him to sit still at least, she was tired, she wanted to rest some more. But he only sat still for a short time; soon enough he was casting about for diversion. The window beside him was made of two long panes, the upper of which slid down, though whatever latch or catch should have held it was broken, and we had lodged bits of paper in the corners to hold it open. He reached up, curling his fingers around the top edge, and hauled himself to his feet, standing on the bench so that his head was above the lowered pane; he stared out over the fields we passed, his view unencumbered by the clouded glass. The train had picked up speed, and his hair was pushed about in the moving air. He began playing a game, turning his head quickly and repeatedly from right to left, focusing his sight on an object and following it as we passed; it was something I had done, too, staring out of windows on long trips in the car. Poor boy, I thought, he had nothing at all to do, no toys or books, though perhaps he was too young for books, and with the prospect of many hours to fill. He turned away from the window, facing the back wall, and reached up toward the metal rack where we had placed our luggage. Then, taking the edge of the rack in both hands, he lifted himself up, his right leg striking out for the window, seeking purchase. This woke his grandmother, who grabbed the leg nearest her and tugged on it, saying *Dolu*, down, saying it again when he dropped to the seat but remained standing. Sit down, she said, you're bothering these people, they want to read, and it was true that we had stopped reading, having turned to look instead at the two of them; but I didn't feel bothered, he was more interesting than my book.

I'm bored, he said, *skuka mi e*, it's a long trip, I want to do something. His grandmother sighed. It's not so long, she said, other children manage to sit and to be good. I'll never sit, the boy cried, squaring his shoulders, and he repeated the word never, *nikoga*, separating each of the syllables, throwing them like little punches in the air. I laughed, I couldn't help it, and the man across from me laughed too; even the grandmother smiled, it was too charming to resist. The boy looked surprised at our laughter, as if he had forgotten about us, and then he glanced at each of us in turn with his enormous smile, thrilled with the impression he had made. Only my mother was left out, and she reached urgently across to grip my arm, asking what he had said, wanting to know before the moment passed. And then she smiled too, looking first at the boy and then his grandmother, laying her hands in her lap and settling back against the bench in a peculiar way she had, as if it were all just too much for words. He's a sweet boy, she said then, looking at the grandmother, who smiled back at her but shook her head, saying she was sorry, she didn't speak any English. I translated what my mother had said, and the woman looked at me, a little surprised. You speak Bulgarian, she said, almost a question, and then, when I had wagged my head from side to side, Well, she said, he can be sweet and still be bad. But she was pleased, and she looked at my mother while I translated, smiling and nodding her head a little. There was a camaraderie among us now, a warmth that made us more than strangers, and the boy felt it too, I thought, so that his sense of his kingdom spread from the little seat, expanding to encompass the entire compartment. At several points during our ride, the man across from us had interrupted his reading to take a camera from the backpack beside him and step into the corridor, snapping photos through the large windows there. The boy had watched this with interest, and now, as the man took his camera out again, he went to stand before him, cocking his head a little. Do you want to see how it works, the man asked, tilting the camera so the boy could see the digital screen surrounded by switches and buttons, and the boy nodded, still shy, and then hopped up onto the bench beside him. Don't bother him, the grandmother said, but the man shook his head at this, saying it was fine, he didn't mind, and he and the boy examined the camera for a few minutes, scrolling through the photos, and then, with the grandmother's blessing, they stepped together into the corridor, where the windows offered more expansive views.

He's my daughter's child, the woman said to us, I took him to the seaside for a week, all he did was run and play, I thought he would sleep on the train, he usually does. I shook my head in sympathy, saying that it was a long trip, it was hard for a child, and really he was being very good. Is this your mother, the woman asked then, and I said yes, saying too that it was her first time in Bulgaria, her first time anywhere outside of the States. Her first time in Europe and you brought her to Bulgaria, the woman said, oh, she must think it is terrible here. I paused to translate for my mother, who gasped and leaned forward, Oh no, she said, it's a beautiful country, I've had a wonderful time. Maybe the sea is nice, the woman allowed, but Sofia—and she cut off her sentence, wrinkling her nose. But she is your mother, the woman said, anywhere she's with you she will be happy. When she heard this, my mother reached over and laid her hand on my arm, saying that was true, that was certainly true, and I felt something twist in me, the motion of some unthinking thing when it is gripped too hard, and I had to resist the urge to pull away. But you live in Bulgaria, the woman asked, what do you do here, and her face brightened with interest when I said I was a teacher, when I named the famous school where I work. *Bravo*, she said, that is the best place, and then she said that her grandchild had started learning English that year, that he had learned songs and already knew his numbers. He was a smart boy, she said, when he wasn't being bad. This last was meant for the boy himself, who had just come back in, he and the man, the boy happy with the camera. He held it to his face (the man kept his own hand on it too), and looked at each of us, using his hand on the lens to twist it first one way and then the other, making us large and small by turns. This man is a teacher, the woman told the child, he teaches English, and she encouraged him to practice his English with me, to show me what he had learned; but the boy turned shy, still smiling but moving his head up and down, a decided no. Come on, I said in Bulgarian, just say a little bit, what words do you know, but he still refused, suddenly demure; he climbed back into his seat and laid his head on the woman's arm. He's shy, the woman said, but really he knows a lot. She told us about the teacher he had had that year at school, a young man, new and full of energy, who played games with the kids, so that they learned without knowing they had been taught. They even put on a show at the end of the year, she said, it was wonderful, all of the students had learned so much. The boy lifted himself up again then, suddenly unshy; I want to say an English word, he said. He wiggled himself to the edge of his seat, the toes of his shoes just touching the floor, and looked around at each of us in turn, as if to make sure we were all watching. Then he threw both of his hands in the air and shouted Kung Fu!, falling back against the seat as he held out the second syllable, turning it into a howl. The woman clicked her tongue, You know better words than that, she said, but the rest of us were laughing again, and again the boy was pleased.

The woman pulled out more food for him then, and the rest of us returned to our reading, though I was hardly reading at all, I was watching the boy with a fascination I didn't understand. There was something electric about him, as he sat chewing his sandwich, looking out the window, a charm beyond mere loveliness. He was still for a while, lulled by food and by the heat, which had grown more intense as the afternoon wore on, but soon he was restless again, climbing up on the bench, then onto the narrow ledge of the armrest, grabbing with both of his hands one of the metal bars of the luggage rack. Get down, his grandmother said sharply, I've already told you, and the boy dropped his hands, not in surrender but to have them free for bargaining. But you don't know what I'm going to do, he protested, his voice full of the injustice of it, I haven't even tried yet. Just wait, just let me try, then see if it's bad, and he made a particular gesture with his hands, curling his fingers slightly and holding them both palm up before him, a pleading gesture, and all at once and with a physical force I understood the source of my fascination with the boy, the reason I had been unable to look away. It was one of Mitko's gestures, I realized, all of the boy's gestures were ones I had seen Mitko use; the boy himself, his long limbs, his slenderness, the peculiar cast of his skin, might have been a small copy of the man, so that I felt I was watching Mitko as a boy, before he had become what he was now. Where had they learned it, I wondered, this repertoire of gestures that made a way of being a man, the talent for friendliness and charm that had always astonished me, with its certainty both of welcome and of the right to whatever it could grasp.

The boy did pull himself up then, showing off his strength, and as his legs flailed in the air the woman grabbed one of them and pulled, which made the boy giggle at first, thinking it was a game. He dropped back down to the little ledge, leaning back against the wall, still smiling, and again brought his hands together in front of him, not pleading now but as if to say see, it was nothing so terrible, how silly you were to worry. But this time the woman snatched one of his hands and yanked it hard, pulling him forcibly into the seat. I said to get down, she said, and it was clear now that she was angry, really angry for the first time in the trip, and it was as much in response to this anger as to any pain she had caused, I thought, that the boy began to weep. He was shocked at first, wide-eyed as if unbelieving that his luck could have run out, and then, though I could see he tried to resist, to act *muzhki*, the tears streamed down. The boy kept wiping them away, using his whole palm, but there were always more, he was outsized in grief as in all other feeling. His grandmother refused to look at him, and I thought, as I had before, how difficult it must be to parent, to divine the discipline or patience by which to make the good seeds grow while plucking out the bad, though maybe there was no real telling them apart. What was charming in the child would not be charming in the man, I thought, remembering Mitko and his bewilderment at my exasperation, his disbelief at every refusal. He had been a child just like this. I glanced at my mother, who looked stricken as she watched the boy weep, her own eyes welling with tears, and I wondered, as I had so often, whether she was the source of my own discontent, whether there was something she could have done that would have made me other than I am. I considered this as I watched her watching the boy, even though I knew it was unfair, that I was lucky to be loved as she loved me.

It was now, as the boy wept, as I watched my mother watch him guardedly, as we all withdrew into our privacies so as to allow the boy his own, that I felt an odd aligning of things, that weird pressure as they found their place and as I found my place among them, my mother and the boy, the hot compartment, my memories of Mitko that came back so fiercely I was wrung by them, by the thought of our last meeting that had left me even after all these months bereft. I pulled my notebook from my bag, wanting to catch this before it faded, scribbling not sentences but impressions, a certain arrangement of things, even as I heard the boy, who had found his voice again, begin his recriminations. He was holding his arm where she had grabbed him, pressing it bent against his chest. *Schupi mi rukata*, he said, you broke my arm, it hurts, you didn't have to pull so hard, but the woman was unmoved, used to his dramatics, I supposed. You should do what I tell you, she said. It's not your train, he responded, less pained now than sullen, you didn't build it, you didn't buy it, using logic like a rampart he could retreat behind, you can't tell me what to do, but none of this merited any reply. There's nothing for me to do, he went on, trying another tack, I don't have anything to play with, I don't have any toys, you won't let me climb, I'm bored, he said, *skuka mi e*. He was on better ground here, I thought, there was some justice in his complaint, though the woman still sat silent. My arm, he said a moment later, as if remembering, it really hurts, and he held it out to her as she took it again in her hand, gently this time, looking concerned, saying Let me see, and then yes, it's very bad, I'm afraid we'll have to cut it off, so that suddenly he was giggling, twisting away as she leaned in, still holding his arm, and began to tickle him. He was all joy now, the tears barely dry on his face, and after a moment at this game he ended draped across her lap, his arms cast about her, a posture so sweet it was almost painful to see, as it was painful to see my mother, who watched them with such longing I had to look away. I could remember a time when we had touched like that, my mother and I, when I sought out her presence and her touch, too, and I wondered where that ease and openness had gone, and why they had been replaced with such stiff discomfort, a sense almost of taboo that kept me from making any answer to her expressions of love. I felt for the first time how cruel I had been, when I had stopped answering her calls and e-mails, which grew increasingly frantic until they fell away. For a time I had been lost to her, and she couldn't have known I would return. They stayed like this for some time, the woman and the boy, with his arms around her and her hands resting on his back.

I lost myself then, writing my notes, so that it was a few moments before I became aware that the boy was watching me; he had pushed himself from his grandmother's lap and was sitting upright, and there was an intensity to his looking, a gravity of desire. I want to write too, he told his grandmother, and while she looked in her bag for a pen, he leaned forward and shyly, as if she might object, drew from the metal bin one of the cards my mother had discarded from her magazines, and then, when she nodded at him and smiled, a second and a third. He settled back, and holding the cards on his lap he began to write, in large block capitals copying out the three words, BUSINESS REPLY MAIL, again and again, practicing the alphabet, I realized, the letters uncertain in his childish hand, a Cyrillic Б replacing the Latin as often as not. I can't say why it affected me as it did, his studiousness, the quiet earnestness with which he worked, but it was heartbreaking, the more so when he turned to the woman and said When I'm finished, he will read it, inclining his head toward me. Maybe now that I saw Mitko in the boy, any future I could imagine for him gave me something to grieve. Should he fail in his studies, or should he find after them there were no jobs to be had, should he turn, like Mitko, to drink or to drugs, thwarting his grandmother's hopes, there was the lost promise of the bright boy before me. But if the boy made the most of that promise, if he left Bulgaria (where there is no future, my students tell me again and again, where there is only the narrowing horizon of diminished expectations), if he thrived beyond anything his grandmother hoped, then there was the thought, unbearable to me, of what Mitko might have been. By the third paper card the boy's writing had lost its shape altogether, softening and flattening out until it was just a wavy line across the page. As the train slowed in its approach to Plovdiv, where my mother and I would spend the night—I wanted her to see the beautiful old city, the ornate wooden houses climbing the hills—he held up this last card with its scribbles for me to read. That must be a language I don't know, I said, smiling, I can't read it, and he seemed satisfied, he grunted and said *Tova e ispanski*, that's Spanish, making me laugh again. You're very smart, I said, as his grandmother shook her head, it's good to know so many languages. My mother and I were standing now, gathering our things, lifting our large bags from the rack, and I found I didn't know how to say goodbye to the boy. I wanted to tell him to study, to work hard, above all to study his English, which he would be helpless without; it was his best chance, I wanted to say, but that's the kind of thing one can never say, there's no way to say it, or no way for it to be heard. And so instead I opened a small pocket of my bag, telling him I wanted to give him something, something you couldn't find in Bulgaria, I said, and I handed him a drugstore peppermint from a packet my mother had brought over for me. It was my favorite candy when I was a child, and I was glad beyond words at the pleasure it gave him when he twisted off the plastic wrapper and popped it in his mouth. Then the train stopped, and my mother and I moved into the corridor, clumsy with our bags and with the prospect of being alone together. As we joined the line of people getting off at the last stop before Sofia, I looked once more at the little boy, whom I felt I would never forget, though maybe it wasn't exactly him I would remember, I thought, but the use I would make of him. I had my notes, I knew I would write a poem about him, and then it would be the poem I remembered, which would be both true and false at once, the image I made replacing the real image. Making poems was a way of loving things, I had always thought, of preserving them, of living moments twice; or more than that, it was a way of living more fully, of bestowing on experience a richer meaning. But that wasn't what it felt like when I looked back at the boy, wanting a last glimpse of him; it felt like a loss. Whatever I could make of him would diminish him, and I wondered whether I wasn't really turning my back on things in making them into poems, whether instead of preserving the world I was taking refuge from it. The doors opened, the line began to move, and I saw that the boy was already clambering into the seats we had left, claiming a new space as his own. And then my mother and I stepped off the train into the evening air, nearly gasping in relief at its freshness.

I must have been sleeping deeply, one night that spring, I must have been in a state beneath dreams or any kind of thought, when suddenly I bolted awake. Just for an instant, I felt what I had felt a few weeks before, when in the dead of night there was a violent jolt and shuddering, a movement that violated not just my sense of physical law but some deeper certainty I had taken for granted. I was pinned to my bed by an animal fear as the world shifted with a sound I had never heard before, a deep grinding thunder and the sound of alarms, all the cars of my neighborhood shrieking their warnings, a bewildering cacophony of patterns and tones. It was the strongest earthquake to strike Bulgaria in a century, the papers would say the next morning, though really it had only been of a middling strength. In Sofia the *blokove* had swayed but none had fallen, and there wasn't much damage beyond broken windows and cracked facades; even in the villages only the oldest structures collapsed. There was one death, the articles said, an old woman whose heart stopped at the shock of it. It was the first earthquake I had ever experienced, and the first time I had known that absolute disorientation and helplessness, the first time I had felt in that incontrovertible way the

minuteness of my will, so that underlying my fear, or coming just an instant after it, was total abandon, a feeling that
wasn't entirely unpleasant, a kind of weightlessness. It was
the noise that made me feel that fear again, just for a moment, and then I was on my feet as I realized the sound that
had woken me wasn't a calamity, but someone pressing again
and again the whirring chime of my door, while at the same
time striking the door itself, not knocking but pounding,
quickly and heavily. I knew who it was, of course, though he
had stayed away for many weeks. I had promised R. I wouldn't
let him in again if he returned, You can't speak to him, he had
said, if you speak to him, if you give any sign to him at all,
he will come back; he has to stop existing for you, he said,
using almost those words. But what could I do, I thought as
I moved to the door, calling out to stop the noise, which must
already have woken the neighbors and which soon would
draw them out, in curiosity or anger; what could I do when
he was constrained by so little, the man on the other side of
the door, who kept up his noise despite my calling to him
from the hall, or perhaps he hadn't heard me over that noise,
since at the first motion of my hand on the key it stopped
all at once, as if now he were ready to be patient. When I
turned the heavy tumblers in their grooves and then the
handle, intending to open the door just slightly, a weight was
applied from the other side, and as I stepped back quickly,
almost falling, I thought maybe he wasn't alone, that he
had come finally to see through the threats he had made in
Varna.

But it wasn't that at all, I saw when Mitko came in, not
stepping but stumbling, moving past me in a strange sidelong way, as if his body were oddly weighted and pulling
him to one side; he wasn't a threat to anyone, a wind could
blow him over. He didn't stop to shake my hand or remove
his shoes or say anything at all, but with his sidelong lurch-

ing movement went into the main room and fell onto the couch. I stood with the door open for a moment, reluctant to close it, as if there were still a chance for what had blown in to blow out, as though he might change his mind and leave before a new revelation emerged, some new drama. I was listening for my neighbors, too, for any opening doors; I would apologize for the noise, in English or Bulgarian, depending on which doors opened. I would say that my friend was drunk, which was true; when he moved past me I had been struck by a strong smell of beer, the kind that comes in two-liter bottles, the cheapest kind. But there was no sign of anyone, the hallway was quiet, and so I did close my door, having no other choice, unless it were to close it behind rather than in front of me, to step out into the hallway and away, which of course was no choice at all.

Mitko was sitting at the end of the couch, though perhaps sitting isn't the word for his slumped-over posture, his body tilted to one side like a listing boat. He had shrugged off his jacket and left it lying crumpled behind him, an uncharacteristic gesture, given the care with which he usually treated his things. He pulled one knee half onto the seat and turned, a welcoming posture, I thought, an invitation for me to sit beside him. His shoulders and back were bowed forward and his head was tilted up at a strange angle, as if he were studying something at a middle height, the cupboards above the sink, perhaps, though as I approached and then sat at the other end of the couch, keeping as much distance between us as I could, I saw he wasn't studying anything. His eyes were moving eerily, rolling uselessly in his head, as if disjointed from his will, and his neck was not merely tilted up but straining. It was a posture of agony, I thought, and though clearly he was drunk, drunker than I had ever seen him, drunker than I had ever seen anyone, I thought surely he must have taken something too, some substance the effects of which were beyond my acquaintance with such things. He looked terrible, even thinner than before, so that the clothes he had always worn tight hung loose against his frame; and there was something else as well, less easy to pinpoint but just as alarming, some subtly wrong color to his skin that made it difficult not to pull away from him.

I didn't recoil, but it was as though he had seen the impulse as he reached over and took one of my hands in his. I had noticed his hands moving oddly, the fingers rubbing against one another in a strange way, as though surprised to find such close neighbors, and now he clasped my hand tightly, taking it in both of his, and kneaded it, squeezing so hard the knuckles popped. *Dobre li si*, I said to him, are you all right; clearly he wasn't but I had to say something. He shook his head quickly, not in answer but as if to shake off my voice, and I thought he made an effort to look at me; his eyes stopped their rolling for a moment, they seemed to seek me out, but then began their motion again. He held my hand quietly for a while, still kneading it in his strange way, grinding the joints of my fingers against one another, so that I had to squeeze back to avoid pain. And then he started speaking, though not to me, exactly, or to anyone; he began to repeat a single phrase, which even though it was short I didn't catch at first, both because his speech was slurred and because it was so odd, a statement of counterfact, *Men me nyama*, he said, the three words again and again, *men me nyama, men me nyama*, I'm gone, it means, or I'm not here, literally there's no me, an odd construction I can't quite make work in English. For a moment I thought he was singing a pop song from the previous summer, "Dim da me nyama," which is impossible to translate but the idea is of disappearing in smoke, like a car spinning its tires before shooting off, maybe, or like the running bird in the cartoon. It was a rap song, and the chorus repeated the title again and again,

rhythmically, almost like a chant, which was why I thought
Mitko was singing it for a moment, his own words matched
it so closely, *men me nyama, men me nyama.* I almost smiled at
his drunkenness before I realized that he wasn't singing at
all, and that his eyes, which hadn't stopped their weird motions, had welled with tears. What is it, I said then, what does
that mean, I don't understand, and at this Mitko stopped his
chant, snapped it off as if he were biting it with his teeth,
and almost angrily he said *Nishto ne razbirash*, you don't understand anything. Okay, I said soothingly, I don't understand, tell me, but even before I could soothe him his anger,
if it was anger, had melted away, had become a more agitated
pressing of my hands. *Dnes sum tuk*, he said, *a utre men me
nyama*, today I'm here, tomorrow I'm gone, and then he took
up his weird chant again. It was a charm against something,
I thought, though maybe that was giving it too much meaning, maybe it was less than a charm, like a stone one turns
in one's hand, not for any purpose but for the feel of it.

Then he stopped his chant and said my name, or not my
name but that syllable he used to approximate it, since
my name was unpronounceable in his language; he had
tried to say it at first but each time stumbled over sounds he
couldn't make, the intricate shapes that made him shake his
head in bemusement. I had felt this myself with R.; the English version of his name is common enough, but it sounded
strange in Portuguese, and though I practiced pronouncing
it endlessly and though I'm good at learning languages, each
time I said his name R. would laugh, and so I stopped using
it, I used other names instead, private names I had invented
and so could never mispronounce. The syllable Mitko used
was a private name too, it was his alone, and he said it now as
if to bring me into focus, saying it a second time and a third,
and then, *Shte umra*, he said, I'm going to die, they say I'm
going to die, and at his own words the tears that had welled

up spilled over, streaming down his cheeks. He let go of me to wipe them away, using the palms of both hands, and then he held his hands over his eyes, rocking his whole body back and forth now that his hands were still. Mitko, I said, reaching over to place my hand on his back, unsure what to do with it now that it was free, Mitko, what do you mean, who says this, and he answered, still rocking, *Lekarite*, the doctors, they say my kidneys and my liver don't work, they say I will only live a year. Mitko, I said again, Mitko, and maybe the single syllable oh, I'm not sure what I intended it to mean. But how, I found myself saying, from what, thinking that it couldn't be the syphilis, which should have taken years to do its work, even if he hadn't taken the drugs I gave him money for, gave him money for twice over; but he shook his head at this sharply when I asked him, *Ne*, he said, *ne*, and then he said nothing else. I remembered the months he had spent in the hospital years before, something do with his liver, though he never really spoke of it, avoiding it as he did so much of his past; hepatitis, I had thought, which I knew was rampant here and against which I had long been immunized. Or maybe it wasn't that either, maybe it was just the endless alcohol he drank, though he was still so young, I don't know. And then I remembered what he had said that night in the McDonald's, just before the encounter I had thought of so often since, with longing and excitement and remorse so tightly bound there was no picking them apart, when he said that the drugs we were both to take were dangerous for him. Maybe he hadn't been able to walk away from the illness unscathed, as I had; maybe that was what I meant by that syllable I repeated, oh, the unfairness of the luck I couldn't regret, even as already it was opening up some great space between us, an even greater distance than had existed before. And so I said his name a third time, calling to him across that open space, though he didn't respond, he just kept rocking back and forth, already unreachable.

I want to go, he said then, and heaved himself off the couch. He swayed for a moment and stumbled, catching himself by throwing out first one leg and then, as he began to fall forward, the other. Maybe he had stood up too quickly and was dizzy, in addition to being drunk and whatever else he was, and in this odd, almost falling way he moved from the main room to the hallway. I stood too, unsure whether I should stop him or be grateful the ordeal had been so brief. Now that I knew or thought I knew I would finally be rid of him I didn't want him to go, and I was almost happy to see him turn away from the door, walking or stumbling instead down the hallway to my bedroom. I got up to follow, and watched as he collided with the bed and then fell down upon it, as if he were feeling his way in the dark and had been surprised by it. He lay for a moment and then pushed himself up, swaying before half falling again. He stayed then in a half-sitting, half-lying posture, his hands still working, I saw, gripping and releasing the light blanket I had been sleeping under. I stood at the doorway, watching, unsure whether I should go to him; the bed was a dangerous place, with its memories of what we had done there. But then as if his strength gave out Mitko let himself fall, drawing his legs onto the bed (he hadn't removed his shoes, I saw them muddy the sheets), and then he pulled his knees to his chest and again began to weep, but quietly this time, the tears sprang and his face closed in on itself but his mouth opened and shut without making a sound. I did go to him then, I went to the bed and lay beside him and put my arm on his shoulder, not embracing him but offering him comfort, I hoped, a sign of my presence though I touched him nowhere else, and immediately he seized my arm with his and pulled it to his chest, which rose and fell as he gasped in his silent weeping. And he didn't just pull me to him, he rolled back as well; I had kept a space between us but he pressed against me, the whole length of his back against my front. I tightened my arms around him, holding him as he wept, and he reached one of his legs through mine and pulled me tight, so that I felt his body all along my own, his body that had been, in however partial or compromised or intermittent my fashion, beloved to me. As I pressed my face to his neck and breathed him in, his scent sour with sweat and alcohol, it seemed impossible it could dissolve, simply dissolve, this form I had known so intimately with my hands and my mouth, it was unbearable that this body so dear to me should die. But though I held him more tightly the space that had opened up between us remained, and I knew I would stay on the other side of it, the side of health, I knew I wouldn't stay with Mitko and face the death he faced; I know it's everywhere, that it's an illusion we ever look anywhere else, but as long as I could believe it I would pretend to look away. Love isn't just a matter of looking at someone, I think now, but also of looking with them, of facing what they face, and sometimes I wonder whether there's anyone I could stand with and watch what I wouldn't watch with Mitko, whether with my mother, say, or with R.; it's a terrible thing to doubt about oneself but I do doubt it.

Even so, I lay beside him, I held him as he held my arm, embracing it against his chest. When he had calmed he began to speak, and his hands, which had been still as he wept, started to knead me again where they gripped me, taking up again their strange motion. *Obichash li me*, he asked, do you love me, but it wasn't a question; I know you love me, he said, not waiting for me to speak. I know you love me but I can't love you, I'm sorry, you are my friend, he said, *priya-*

tel, that word that could mean so much and so little, you are my friend but *poveche ne moga*, I can't do anything more. Hush, Mitko, I said, it's all right, don't worry, I understand, but he wasn't listening to me, he was speaking for himself, the circling of his thoughts impossible for me to follow. *Gospod go obicham*, he said, and for a moment I thought I must have misunderstood him, he had never spoken of such things before. But he said it again, I love God, *no men ne me obicha*, but God doesn't love me, God loves the strong and I'm not strong, and again he was weeping, speaking at that strange heightened pitch the voice strikes under strain; he loves the strong, he said again and again, repeating it like a chant or a prayer. What are you saying, I said to him, *gluposti*, nonsense, and again I told him to hush, speaking to him as if he were a child, I didn't know how else to speak to him. God loves the strong, he said again, and I'm not strong. *Iskam maika si*, he said then, I want my mother, and again the tears came freely, he had taken my hand and was squeezing it hard. Do you love God, he asked me when he could speak again, do you go to church, and now I didn't try to speak, not knowing how to answer, unable to bring myself to say what I knew would quiet him, though it felt unkind I couldn't make myself say the words.

He squeezed my hand harder, pressing against me, coaxing me, God loves you, he said, you should love God, God believes in you, you should believe in God. All right, I said finally, all right, agreeing with whatever he said, or making the sound of agreement, and then he was silent for a while, and increasingly still. He was falling asleep, and though I took pleasure in the weight of him beside me I wondered how long he would be there, whether I should wake him, whether I would be able to if I tried. I had no idea what time it was, there was no clock in the room, and though I had gone to bed early I thought it was late now, probably not long before I would have to get ready to teach. Maybe it would be better to wake him now, I thought, before he was sound asleep, it would be unkind to wake him but he couldn't spend the night. I would give him money for a room somewhere else, I decided, but before I could bring myself to rouse him he roused himself. *Ne*, he said sharply, I don't want to sleep, and he let go of my hands to push himself upright again. He sat there hanging his head, propped up by his hands on either side while I kept my own hand on his back, both as a steadying force and also for the touch itself. Soon I wouldn't be able to touch him, I thought, maybe I would never touch him again. *Gladen sum*, he said, I'm hungry, I haven't eaten for a long time. He stood awkwardly, again as if having misjudged the force it took, so that he overshot the mark, as it were, and almost tumbled forward, catching himself by putting his hand out toward the wardrobe door and pressing his fingers on the mirror mounted there, leaving marks I would find myself examining in the days that followed, until the woman who comes to clean my apartment wiped them away. Mitko moved in his lurching way out of the room but I stayed where I was, lying in a half-raised position as I heard the refrigerator door open and the noise of things being taken out. A few minutes later, he called out that single syllable that was his name for me, that called me to myself or rather to that self I was with him, and I got up slowly to join him.

He was more lucid now, the effects of alcohol or whatever else wearing away, or maybe he was refreshed by his few minutes of sleep. He was sitting upright, perched on the very edge of the couch, leaning forward between his knees, having laid out before him a banana and a cup of yogurt, a spoon and beside this a bottle of milk. *Ela tuka*, he said, come here, and I sat beside him again, closer this time. *Trugvam si*, he said, I'm going, I'm not going to bother you, I just want to eat something first, and I told him not to worry, he wasn't bothering me at all. I had checked the time after he left the bedroom, waiting until then to pick up my phone where it lay on the table beside the bed, and I was surprised to see it was early still, not even midnight, my sleep though it had been deep had been brief. Mitko picked up the banana he had placed on the table, and with exaggerated care began to unpeel it, drawing each long strip down slowly, as if every movement required the greatest attention. It was as though he had lost the sense of his body in space, I thought, that unthinking knowledge we have; it was as though nothing could be assumed but must be carefully measured out. His eyes weren't rolling anymore but they weren't quite focused either, he didn't track the banana as he brought it to his lips and bit into the tip of it. He turned slightly to me, holding the banana out in offering. Eat, he said gravely, speaking in English, and when I didn't eat he said it again, pressing the white flesh against my lips. But I don't want to eat, I said, though it wasn't simply that; I was unnerved by the seriousness with which he stared at me, stared or didn't quite stare with his unfocused eyes, and I didn't want to participate, it felt sacramental somehow, like a ritual by which I would be bound. But Mitko ignored what I said, pressing the fruit more urgently against my lips, so that I had to turn away. I don't want it, I said, but he hushed me, blowing his breath between his teeth; *Vizh*, he said, look, and then he brought the banana back to his lips. I eat, he said, speaking again in English, and then holding the banana to my face again, now you eat. But again I turned away, and he returned his hand to his lips. *Dnes sum tuka*, he said, speaking again the words he had made his chant, today I'm here, I eat, do you understand, I eat. *Razbiram*, I said, and again he snapped back at me *Nishto ne razbirash*, you don't understand anything. But then his voice softened, as it had before, I understand you, he said, but you don't understand me, and he looked at me again with such sadness that I did eat, finally taking the gift he had offered, though I could barely swallow, my gorge rose at the sweetness of it.

Good, he said in English, good, and then he set the banana down half-eaten, carefully folding the skin back over the flesh. He picked up the yogurt then, a cheap flavored brand, and after carefully peeling back the aluminum cover halfway (centimeter by centimeter, again as if measuring the force it took) he brought the cup to his lips and took two large mouthfuls, not spooning it out but drinking it. He turned to the milk again, and holding it in one hand and the yogurt in the other, he began to pour the milk into the cup, slowly, as if he were determined to maintain the thinnest possible ribbon of liquid, a process made difficult by the fact that his hands were trembling, both of them, as they always did when he was drunk. *Mite*, I said, using my own name for him, his nighest name, I thought, or as nigh as I could come, shortened as if for a child, *Mite*, is there nothing they can do, is there no treatment? Without looking away from his task, as though any break in concentration would disrupt the delicate process, he brought his head up and then down, a decisive gesture, *Ne*, he said, *nishto*. I wondered why this was so, whether because of his condition or because of the expense of whatever was needed to treat it, even here where such things are so much cheaper, and I let myself imagine taking it on, the impossible task of saving him, for a single breath I imagined it, and then I let it go.

He set down the milk and yogurt, and having peeled the foil top the rest of the way off he began stirring the mixture with a spoon. He was making some variant of *airan*, I realized, the watered yogurt that everyone loves in Bulgaria. *Mite*, I said again, I will help you, I will give you money to go back to Varna. *Ne iskam pari*, he said, I don't want money, and he took my hand in his again, squeezing it, though not with the same force as before. I came because you are my friend, he said, many people say they're your friend but they aren't, they're with you and then when you need them they're gone. But you are a real friend, he said, *istinski*, you have helped me many times, and I thought but that isn't what I've done, remembering those transactions that had nothing to do with help, I was claiming him the only way I could. But I didn't say this, I said I'm glad for that, looking into his eyes that looked at me so earnestly and yet weren't looking at me at all. Let me help you now, I said, you should go back to Varna, you should be with your mother. At this his eyes softened still further, and I watched them fill with tears. Mitko nodded, he would take the money, and I wondered what urge had been satisfied in pretending he might not. *Istinski priyatel*, he said again, letting go of my hand and turning back to his drink.

But I am your friend too, he said then, the tone of his voice shifting as he poured more milk into the cup, do you know how good a friend I've been? Other people, when they've seen us together, they've said Mitak—which was another one of his names, people here have many nicknames, I had seen others use it with him on Skype or hookup sites but I had never used it myself; it sounded hard to me, Mitak, I never felt it would summon the person I wanted him to be with me. Mitak, they've said, what are you doing with that guy, why are you hanging out with that faggot, and he used the word *pederast*, here as elsewhere it's the preferred term of abuse. There are other words for what he said, of course, but *pedal* or *obraten* wouldn't have struck with the same force, I would have had to translate them, however quickly; words in a foreign language never wound us like words in the language to which we're born. But when

I heard this word, *pederast*, I drew away from him slightly and grew very still. But *ne ne vikam az*, he went on, I say he's not a faggot, I tell them leave him alone, *toi e hetero*. He was stirring the yogurt in its little cup as he said this, staring not at me but at it, his eyes still unfocused though he was more lucid than I had thought, I realized, lucid enough to make his threats, since I knew it was a threat he was making. Why are you saying this, Mitko, I asked, giving up our private names, why are you saying this to me? He shrugged a little, still stirring the mixture of yogurt and milk, pointlessly now; maybe the motion was like his chant, a rhythm he had fallen into, something he did for the feel of it. There are bad people, he said, speaking in the abstract as he always did when making his threats, gesturing to that gallery of faces or masks any of which he might choose to put on, though for now he let them hang. There are bad people who might say what you are, he said, they might not keep your secrets, they might make trouble, he said, and as he spoke a deeper sadness came over me, not at the betrayal this implied but at how futile it was, that it was the only threat he could make, or that he thought it was a threat at all. It was a threat in a different world, in his world perhaps but not in mine. But Mitko, I said, speaking gently, not in fear but in pity, I am an open person, I don't have these secrets, everyone knows what I am, and I used his formula though it made me uneasy, *tova koeto sum*. Everyone, he said, incredulous, at the College too, your colleagues, your students? Of course, I said as if it could never be otherwise, from the first day I've told them, everyone knows, and as he looked down, shrugging his shoulders again, I felt a strange disappointment, as if I regretted my own safety, as if I missed the threat that lay now out of his reach.

  Mite, I said, using again my favorite name for him, his nighest name or the nighest to me, I'm sorry, it's time for you to go, and as I spoke the words I found that I was sorry, knowing that I would truly be rid of him now. Yes, he said, agreeing, *trugvam si*, but he didn't get up to go; he remained perched on the edge of the couch, his hands on the cup of yogurt he had emptied. I got up and took my wallet from my coat, which was hanging beside the door. The bus to Varna would be thirty leva, or had been not long before, so I took out twice that, and then a little more, and folded the notes until they were a tight coil in my palm. Here, I said, holding this out to him, this will get you to Varna, and there's money for food. He looked at the money I held out but didn't move to take it, as if his unfocused gaze didn't quite recognize what it saw. Here, I said again, you should go to Varna, you should be with your mother. He nodded at this, he wiped his hands on his jeans and then took the money from me and stood up. He was visibly better now, he wasn't quite steady but he didn't stumble. *Mersi*, he said, nothing more, as he slid the money into his pocket. Then he turned and carefully picked up his crumpled jacket, putting it on slowly, not just out of a need to manage his resources, I thought, but out of a reluctance to leave, so that even as he said again *Trugvam si* he made no movement toward the door. He went to the refrigerator instead, pulling it open and peering inside. I'm still hungry, he said, I'll just fry an egg before I go, *pet minuti*, he said, five minutes. But I stepped toward him and put my hand on his shoulder. Mitko, I said, I'm sorry, I have to sleep, you can eat somewhere else, you have enough for that. And again I did feel sorry, I felt cruel forcing him to leave, though I had fed him and given him money. What would it mean to do enough, I wondered, as I had wondered before about that obligation to others that sometimes seems so clear and sometimes disappears altogether, so that now we owe nothing, anything we give is too much, and now our debt is beyond all counting.

Dobre, he said, straightening up, and then once more, *trugvam si*. He took a few steps toward the door before he paused again, turning to face me. I'm okay now, he said, at first I thought referring to his recovered lucidity, now that the effects of alcohol and of whatever else he had taken were wearing off; but then he stepped closer, saying again *Veche sum dobre*, and as he placed his hand on my waist I understood what he was offering. I let him pull us together and press his pelvis to mine so that I felt his cock again, and for a moment I allowed my response, the flood of excitement that only he could make me feel. But then he leaned his head toward mine and I put my hand on his chest, not quite pushing him away but stopping his approach. *Mite*, I said, and then quickly, lest it seem an invitation or an expression of passion, as perhaps it was, *ne*, I said, and then said it again, *ne*. He didn't argue, but he held me a moment longer, rubbing himself against me, grinding against the hardness that was already evident, as if to reassure himself of the effect he had. He was going, he said again, just a moment, and then before I could protest he went to the refrigerator and pulled out another little cup of yogurt. I can take this, he said, not really asking, and I said yes, of course. Then he was at the door again, and this time he did hold out his hand, returning to the rituals he had neglected on arrival. We will never see each other again, he said, never again, smiling slightly, and then, still gripping my hand, as if to keep me from pushing him away, he leaned forward and pressed his lips to mine, not passionately, though mine softened to receive whatever he would give. It was a brief kiss, it lasted a moment, and then he turned and opened the door, leaving me to close it again behind him.

I turned off the lights, wanting to be in darkness or near darkness, it's never truly dark in Mladost, it's only ever twilight with the lights from the street and from the windows of neighboring buildings; and then I crossed back through the main room and stepped out onto the balcony. It was a crisp night, with a spring chill so different from fall or winter, not in its temperature but in the quality of the air, its softness or tenderness, what has always seemed to me like its welcome. It was late but not terribly late, the moon was in the middle of the sky, the only natural light where it hung above the *blokove*. I could hear the traffic on Malinov, and there were two cars coming down my own street, one of which pulled into a gap at the curb to park, drawing itself up on the sidewalk and letting its lights go dark. I heard the closing of the building's door down below, the loud sound it made when pushed open and allowed to swing back freely, a discourteous sound, and then Mitko came into view, walking not quickly but with purpose, not steadily but without risk of tumbling over. He was shaking the cup of yogurt, holding it close to his ear as if fascinated by the sound it made. Ahead of him, the car doors opened, and a young couple stepped out, fashionably dressed, returning from dinner, I supposed. The woman closed her own door and then opened the one behind, bending down to occupy herself with a child, extracting it from its buckles and straps and then rising up again with it in her arms. It was a little girl, I thought, judging from her clothes rather than from any features I could make out, and she was sleeping, her body was limp in her mother's arms. Mitko slowed his pace as he approached them, looking at the little girl with interest, the yogurt still raised to his ear though he had stopped shaking it, and I saw him lean toward the child a little, saying something, though of course I couldn't make out the words. I had witnessed this many times here, the freedom with which people addressed small children, leaning in as Mitko did now, calling them *milichka*, sweetness, as I imagined him doing; no one took offense, as though it were granted that children were a kind of public property, something to be cherished in common. There was a crisis, every few months there were alarming articles in the newspapers about the falling birthrate; though there were many children in my neighborhood the country as a whole was imperiled, people couldn't afford children, or they saw no point in having them, and as everyone who has the chance flees abroad—like my own students, I thought, who are so eager to escape—the population declines and the warnings in the papers grow more strident and the nation itself becomes a little less real, fading away, some fear, to nothing. There's no hope for it, some of my students have said, not in class but in private, whispering as though it shouldn't be said out loud, it is a dying country. Small children are a shared joy, then, their parents bask in it, the stroked cheeks and *milichka*s, but this mother didn't welcome Mitko's joy at the sight of the child; she turned from him just slightly, not rudely but insistently, as if shielding the girl from his interest, and then the father was beside them, ushering them toward their building's door. Mitko stood for a moment, as if perplexed, and again I was filled with grief for him, seeing him standing alone on the street. He had always been alone, I thought, gazing at a world in which he had never found a place and that was now almost perfectly indifferent to him; he was incapable even of disturbing it, of making a sound it could be bothered to hear. Suddenly I was enraged for him, I felt the anger I was sure he must feel, that futile anger like a dry grinding of gears. But from a distance Mitko didn't seem to feel anything at all; these were only my own thoughts, I knew, they brought me no nearer him, this man I had in some sense loved and who had never in the years I had known him been anything but alien to me. He set off again, shaking the cup of yogurt he had never lowered from his ear, and I watched him until he turned out of sight, headed toward the boulevard and the bus that would carry him away. I stood there for some time, gazing at the corner from which he had vanished. Then I stepped inside, and sitting where he had been just a moment before beside me, I lowered my face into my hands.

ACKNOWLEDGMENTS

An earlier version of the first section of this novel was published as a novella in 2011. Thank you to Keith Tuma, Dana Leonard, and everyone at Miami University Press. Special thanks to David Schloss.

·

Anna Stein created a place in the world for this book by the sheer force of her belief in it. Thank you also to Alex Hoyt, Sally Riley, and Nishta Hurry. I'm grateful to Mitzi Angel for her heroic editing, and to everyone at Farrar, Straus and Giroux for being so welcoming of this novel and its author. Thank you especially to Will Wolfslau for his invaluable help.

·

It has been a privilege to spend the last two years at the Iowa Writers' Workshop. Thank you to Connie Brothers, Deb West, Jan Zenisek, and Kelly Smith. I'm grateful to Lan Samantha Chang for her generous and brilliant teaching, and to the members of her Fall 2013 novel workshop, especially Micah Stack, Novuyo Rosa Tshuma, and D. Wystan Owen. Work on this book was supported by an Iowa Arts Fellowship and a Richard E. Guthrie Memorial Fellowship;

many thanks to the University of Iowa and the Guthrie family for their generosity.

.

For advice and encouragement, thank you to Elizabeth Frank, Kyle Minor, Peter Cameron, Elizabeth Kostova, Honor Moore, Paul Whitlatch, Margot Livesey, Robert Boyers, and Stephen McCauley. For the inspiration of their teaching and example, thank you to Frank Bidart, Kevin Brockmeier, Carolyn Forché, Carl Phillips, Jorie Graham, and James Longenbach. For pointing me toward a title, thank you to Meredith Kaffel. For checking my Bulgarian, thank you to Maria Manahova and Boian Popunkiov.

.

For reading first and final drafts, thank you to Mary Rakow, Ilya Kaminsky, and Ricardo Moutinho Ferreira.

.

It is impossible to imagine my life without Alan Pierson and Max Freeman, my chosen family. Finally, thank you to Luis Muñoz, *por una canción largamente esperada*.